Shadow Play

A.R. Miller

Mass-Market Edition - 2016

ISBN-10: 0-9914933-6-2
ISBN-13: 978-0-9914933-6-4

The Fey Creations Series

Disenchanted
Unenchanted
Re-enchanted
Shadow Play

This one's for The King and Soda Pop.
Forever immortalized on the page.

Chapter 1

I watch my sandaled foot scrape Var Royd's expensive rug, toes digging into the lush pile, working it one way then the other. Not only do I seem contrite, but I don't have to look into the sea-and-sky-colored eyes of an angry god. An angry god who's also my boss.

"You will answer the phone when I call—"

"I was—"

Rising from his chair, Var slams his hands on the desktop. "Indisposed, washing your hair, in the shower, your excuses read like a handbook for avoiding male suitors."

A snicker, badly concealed as a cough, earns me a nasty glare and I go back to concentrating on the rug and my glittery pedicure.

"I am not a male suitor calling on you, I am your employer. Unless you are dying, I do not care what you are doing when the phone rings. Answer the damn thing."

This isn't the first go around we've had since I took the job of Shadow, nor will it be the last. His Lordship simply can't get it through his thick skull that I'm not going to drop everything and answer the damn phone every time he calls. Hel, I probably won't answer if I'm not busy, unless I feel like it. What's he going to do? Fire me?

I already know he won't deliberately kill me, not without knowing what my Talents would do in death. That's the reason Einen—the former Shadow—is locked away and not dead: fear. Fear that we would be more powerful than Var in his half-assed godhood status. That's right, I said it, Lord Ingvar, aka Frey, isn't running at full power. If he was he wouldn't be so reliant on the three S's, Shadow, Sword, and Shield. Too bad I can't convince Teiran and Ric that we're the one's in control when push comes to shove.

The only thing keeping me from total rebellion is the threat of the returned embrace of my killer collar. Restraints can be fun in the right situation, but there's nothing fun about that one. I do not want to be the daisy that gets its head popped off because my Talents went haywire. That's what makes the collar the perfect deterrent, I won't purposely kill myself to find out if my Talents can regenerate me.

I nod, keeping my head down and eyes on the floor. Working with gods, you quickly learn when to push, when to pull, and when to keep your mouth shut. It doesn't matter if they need you, there's always a point of no return. I haven't hit that point yet, and don't intend on trying today.

Next to me, Teiran's a ball of nerves. I don't need to be an empath to know he's pissed off, I can see his hands balled into fists out of the corner of my eye and hear the change in his breathing as Var berates me. Then again, Teiran is always pissy. I don't think it's a döckâlfar—or dark elf—thing, I'm betting it has something to do with his being a helhound. Someday, I'll get the whole story of how that happened.

Always the diplomat, Ric clears his throat and breaks the awkward silence. I'm not sure if it's just Ric's nature or if it has something to do with his liosâlfar—light elf—heritage. "Lord Royd, perhaps you could tell us why you have summoned us."

"This"—a forceful finger plants itself on the newspaper setting on his desk—"is why I have summoned you."

Ric takes a step toward the desk, and gently slides the paper from under Var's finger. His brow furrows as he reads. *Do not push him today, Keely, his patience will be shorter than usual.*

I feel rather than hear the words forming in my head. Ric's ability to push his thoughts into my head is disconcerting. I take comfort he can't read mine, unless I push the thoughts toward him. If he could, there would be complications I can't deal with right now.

To a rather large extent, I trust Ric, but if he could read my thoughts there'd be nothing but his honor stopping him from telling Var what I'm thinking. And I highly doubt he would, or even could, go against a direct order. Honor is something Ric doesn't take lightly and he's honor bound to serve his Lord Royd above all else.

I'm kind of surprised he hasn't told Var about my dealings with the goddess of the underworld, Hel. His silence on the subject is one reason I *do* trust him. I tip my head down, hoping he takes it as a sign I *heard* and promise to keep my lips zipped. As he hands the paper to Teiran, I get a glimpse of the article that has everyone in a tizzy.

I expect a scathing expose, but it's a letter from the editor, Haydn Koehler. He's siding with the Coalition For A Magical Tomorrow in the accusations against Var for discrimination against Enchants. Not very impartial on the press side, but it is an editorial piece, not factual news.

The CFMT is a hippy-dippy community of Ens and Uns who preach tolerance and equality for all. I don't buy into their glittery, rose-scented, unicorn-fart sentiments. Everyone knows unicorns don't fart glitter and it sure as hel doesn't smell like roses.

Like everyone else on the planet, members of the CFMT want something to bitch about. Some people just go out of their way to find that something and when they do, they blow it out of proportion and scream a little louder than everyone else. Yes, some things need to be brought out into the open, but most of those things ultimately get used to tear someone or something else down. In the end, the only thing that matters to the loudest voice is their own agenda. There is no equality in that. And don't get me started on tolerance.

Discrimination has been around since the beginning of time, but the Unveiling in the 80's gave the world someone new to hate: those of us born with magic. The announcement of the existence of everything Unchants considered myth spawned a decade of excess, excitement, and enchantment. As the 90s rolled around, fear reared its ugly head in a big way. Not that I blame Uns for hating us, it's natural to fear what you don't understand. We also hate what we can't have. This goes for both sides.

I've never met Haydn Koehler, but I hear he's *very* persuasive, something that comes in handy working for the press. I'm not sure if it's his Talent, his boyish good looks, or his tongue is just that smooth. The ginger-haired editor can stir the most passive of souls into action. Somehow, he knows the right buttons to push to get people riled up and right now he has my new boss riled like I've never seen him.

I'd like to tell Var he brought this on himself with the evasive rejection of insurance coverage to Ens, but I don't think it would be prudent. Not answering my phone is a small thing, telling him he could have avoided being called out is way on the other side of the pissed-o-meter.

Instead, I open my mouth and something almost as stupid tumbles out. "What do you want us to do about it?"

Teiran's icy grip on my should shut me up, but why stop the stupidity train once it's rolling?

"What? It's a legitimate question. We aren't exactly equipped to handle a bad PR situation."

Head lowered, Ric pinches the bridge of his nose between his fingers. *Keely, stop while you are ahead.*

Choosing to ignore the warnings, I tilt my head to one side and concentrate my attention on Var. "You have people better suited to manage a media problem like this don't you?"

"Yes, Schattenkind, I do and they will handle that portion of the problem. The three of you will attend to it from another angle."

"What angle?" A fist clenches the muscles of my stomach. "You can't have your muscle beat him up, it will only add to the drama, Var."

Laughter. Genuine, tension breaking laughter. "You are correct, it would make the situation irreparable."

"Then what do you expect us to do?"

"I expect you, Schattenkind, to do your job."

My jaw lowers, but nothing comes out and his

smile widens. It's a smile that curdles my blood.

"It is time for you to put your Talents to use. You will be my spy in the CFMT camp, preferably watching over Mr. Koehler himself, by any means necessary."

Chapter 2

Looks like the pseudo romance with Var is over, no more flowers, flattery, and dinners at expensive restaurants. Not that I presumed—or wanted—anything more out of our *relationship*. What I didn't expect was the level he assumes I'll lower myself to.

"A whore, the asshat expects me to play whore."

"That is not what he said."

Spinning around, I face my partners as they hurry to keep up with me through the Des Moines skywalk system. "Really, Ric? Then what would you call it? I believe his words were, 'You will be my spy in the CFMT camp, preferably watching over Mr. Koehler himself.' That doesn't reek of seduction to you?"

Ric's stride slows finally coming to a stop. His mouth gapping and the faintest flush rising under his perpetual golden tan.

Teiran, on the other hand, takes a play from my book and rolls his eyes. "No offense, but your talents of seduction were not the talents Lord Royd was referring to, Miss Fey."

When someone starts a sentence with *no offense*, it's hard not to take offense. It doesn't matter that Teiran is right about which talents Royd was referring to, what matters is my rant. If either of them had a brain in their pretty heads they'd see a rant for what it is and keep their mouths shut until it passes. Damn hoity-toity elves, or possibly it's just men in general, gotta push the subject. "So what you're trying to say is I'm not the seductive type."

"That is not what I said at all, now watch where you are going." He tries to grasp my arm and I jerk away, stumbling into something solid, yet movable. A muffled curse, hot liquid splashes my back, my ankle twists, and I hit the ground. Hard.

Ric kneels in front of me, poking and prodding various body parts. "Are you hurt?"

I nod, shake my head, and shrug all at once. My pride is in the toilet, my hip will be sporting a bruise the colors of '80s glam eyeshadow, the back of my shirt is soaked in what smells like hazelnut with cream and sugar, and my left wrist hurts like hel. The pain isn't as bad as when I broke it running from The Collector, but my memory is a little fuzzy around the edges. There's no telltale bone protruding, but it's hard to tell what's going on under the bracelet. Clenching it to my chest, I wiggle my fingers. Movement is a good sign, right?

Ric reaches toward my wrist then pulls back as I clutch it closer to my body. I'm glad to see there's a mutual understanding between us that this is not the time or place to remove the bracelet Mel gave me.

The owner of Witchy Weeds made the ultimate—or would that be intimate?—sacrifice to help me. She traded a date with a lecherous alchemist to keep Hel's mark hidden from Var. The spells woven into the bracelet also keep Hel from calling me. I owe her big time. Then again, she did help The Sisters, my grandmother and great-aunts, put the block on my Talents. Maybe we're even.

Ric flips his hand over and I take hold with my right, letting him help me to my feet. His arm curls around my waist, steadying my wobbling as I shift the weight from my left side and turn to see who I backed into.

An awkward blond pats spilled coffee from his three-piece, tweed ensemble with a cloth handkerchief. Wow, all he needs is a pair of—he lifts his head and looks directly at me, a big smile taking over his face—horn rimmed glasses. Stuffing the handkerchief into his pocket, without so much as a howdy do to Ric and Teiran, he beelines toward me.

His style choices do little to mask his lack of years, mid-twenties, maybe late. For all I know, he's one of those who's blessed with the perpetual look of youth. What I can tell is there's not a trace of inherent Talent, so either he's really good at masking or he's an Unchant. Although appearances can deceive, I'm placing my bet on Un. His lack of fear is a whole other issue. Not that I expect him to know who or what we are, I find his dismissal of Ric and Teiran curious. I mean, seriously, Teiran's a big intimidating dude—especially for an elf—and Ric's not exactly nonthreatening, clothed in his usual black leather. Not that I don't find a pretty elf in black leather sexy, but that duster ranks up there with tweed on the list of things not to wear in Iowa, in August.

"I'm so sorry for running into you." He takes the cloth out of his pocket and proceeds to try and move behind me.

Turning in a tight circle to keep him and his handkerchief out of my personal space and within my sight. "No worries, I'm the one who wasn't watching where I was going."

"No, no, I was the one not paying attention. If you'll just send me the dry cleaning bill—"

Dry cleaning bill? It's a freakin' tee-shirt and jeans. "Like I said, don't worry about it, I'm the one who should be paying your dry cleaning, your suit took the brunt of our collision. At the very least, I owe you another coffee."

I reach into my pocket and pull out a wadded bill—that turns out to be a one, when straightened—assorted coins, a lint ball and some random hair. It doesn't matter how hard you try and contain it, somehow you end up with every haircut hidden somewhere on your person.

He smiles and shakes his head. "No, the gentleman in me cannot allow you to reimburse me for something that was in no way your fault."

Teiran, clearly annoyed by the whole situation and not caring who knows, grabs hold of my upper arm. "It was an accident, you have both made your peace, and it is time to move on."

"I must agree, we have other appointments to keep." Ric helps steer me down the walkway away from the curious Mr. Tweed.

"Wow, rude much?" I say, when we're safely out of earshot.

"There was nothing rude about what we did, there was an accident, apologies were made, and we moved on. Listening to you two repeatedly offer to clean the other's clothing or pay for coffee is a waste of time. We have more pressing matters at hand."

"Teiran is right, watching the boy flirt with you was becoming painful and would only end in embarrassment for him."

"Flirting? You two think he was flirting with me? The whole incident was pretty much my fault, he was just being polite."

The look between then says they believe otherwise and a glance over my shoulder has me questioning my opinion. Mr. Tweed stands where we left him, hands in his pockets, watching us walk away. His bland expression is anything but flirty or even polite, until he notices me looking and smiles.

Chapter 3

All I want is a few moments of peace and a decadent, caffeinated treat before work. I need to center myself and switch gears from super-secret agent to mild-mannered hairstylist. Secret agent, yeah, right. August's sweltering humidity turns icy as I step inside Midnite Expresso.

The AC isn't the only thing that's ice cold. Everyone's attention turns my way and silence descends. How the hel am I supposed to spy on Hayden Koehler when I can't get a cup of coffee without undue notice? Sure, I'm in The Meadows where everyone knows me, but the whole Collector fiasco has made me… notorious? Or is it my ties with Royd and his triad of stupidity? Couldn't possibly be the confirmation of my shadowy ways. The reason doesn't matter, I stick out like a sore thumb.

"Hey, Keely." Candy waves from behind the counter. "WCM?"

"Yeah, extra-large, on ice."

Ignoring the stares and mumbled comments, I lean against the counter to watch Candy work her magic with the espresso machine.

"Have you heard the news?" She practically yells to be heard over the machine.

"Nope." News in The Meadows equates to gossip, something I pay little to no attention to.

"The mayor told the sheriff get rid of the *over abundance* of pigeons hanging out in town."

"Mourning doves, they're mourning doves, not pigeons."

"Pigeons, mourning doves, whatever, they make a hel of a mess. Extra-large, white chocolate mocha on ice."

She places a tall glass of icy perfection in front of me. I slide some cash toward her, wave away the change, and stab a straw into the container as I walk toward the door. Luckily, they don't know the reason for the *over abundance*. With her inability to call me to her, Hel's sent her spies to keep an eye on me. Get rid of one hairstylist and all the mourning doves would follow.

Back out in the heat, I pause and take a sip of almost instantly diluted WCM. After five and it's still over ninety degrees. This is one of the rare times Teiran's icy attitude would come in handy, keeping me and my drink cool.

I'll give Hel credit, she's smart enough to scatter her minions to all the buildings downtown and not just mine. With the bracelet keeping her from yanking me into her reality, she's relying on the doves to keep her informed. I wonder if she uses the same tactics on her helhound, it would explain Teiran knowing they were Hel's go-betweens. And if that's the case, does she use them to watch over Einen?

Maybe I should march into Helheim and demand she help me find Einen. She'll be so receptive to me ordering her around. I already owe her a favor for healing the wrist I broke escaping from The Collector. A healing that left me permanently sporting her mark, a combination of the runes Ear and Berkana. A mark she uses to call me to her, or punish me for over stepping my bounds. The marked wrist sheathed by a spelled bracelet of platinum, lead, and aluminum—gods know what else—that keeps her from calling—or punishing—me. Yeah, she'll be real receptive to a request for assistance.

A small sports car slows, coming to a stop in front of me and the window lowers revealing a mass of violet-black hair. "Looking for a date? My friend wants to know how much."

"I know what your friend makes, he can't afford me."

Nyssa giggles as Rey pulls her back inside the car and shouts, "Hel, I can afford both of you with my tips alone."

"If that's the case, maybe I should up your chair rental."

"You'll forget before the next contract renewal."

Another car pulls up behind him, blaring its horn.

"See ya inside," yells Nyssa as they speed away.

I wave, waiting my turn to cross the heat drenched asphalt. Gotta love my co-workers, at least the ones at Fey Creations. Nyssa and Rey make the most of life, grasping fun by the horns and making it their bitch. Not that they're irresponsible, quite the contrary, they've just perfected a balance that works for them. Unlike the fourth member of our team, Dara. Fun slipping past her austere shields is a rarity, and right now those shields are tighter and higher than ever. And I'm the reason. Actually, my choice to take the job of Shadow is the reason.

Nyssa and Rey scurry around the corner as I unlock the front door.

Rey skids to a halt beside me. "I win."

"No fair, I'm wearing heels."

"And I thank you for it." He pats her bottom and growls.

She squeals, rubbing her backside as she slips past him. "Ha! I win."

"Do not, I was clearly here first. Right, Keely?"

"Leave me out of it and get inside, Rey." I give him a push inside and lock the door behind us.

"The bet was for who made it in, not to the salon first. I win, fair and square." Nyssa completes the statement by tracing a square between them.

"Yep, that's you, square as they come," Rey comments over his shoulder with a laugh.

She chases after him. "Hey, take that back."

It's like working with children. Children whose ages are multiples of multiples of mine, but children nonetheless. I don't know anyone's true age, they all skirt around the question but take great pleasure in bringing up mine. Even though I'm middle-aged in the human system, my elven heritage makes me a pre-teen at best. Not that that matters, no woman wants to be reminded she's lived through teased flips, hippy straight, Farrah feathered, punk spikes, mall bangs and the Rachel. My only consolation is the nixie, therian, and vampire I hang with are much older, even if they don't act it. Well, Nyssa and Rey don't, Dara acts as if she's been around since the beginning of time. Maybe she has been, considering she served Sekhmet before she became a vamp.

A low whistle sounds over my shoulder. "It's going to be a long night."

I laugh, glancing at Rey's column of the appointment book. "One in a darkened facial room with soft music." Turning the chair, I grin. "It's Horny Harpy night."

A sour lemon expression twists his lean face. "Yeah, but I'll be keeping my eye on the prize - big tips." His jaw tightens. "That's the only thing that keeps me from telling them I'm booked."

Sexual harassment is not just a man on woman thing, men just don't talk about it publicly. Rey doesn't usually do facials, with the exception of Mrs. Daniels and her two best friends. The rest of us have a theory about why they like Rey to do their facials. It involves a sexy man touching them in a candlelit room, leading to us calling them the Horny Harpies. Three past-their-prime, overtly vain Unchants with too much money and time on their hands. Rey may be a flirt, but he knows where to draw the line. Unfortunately, the Horny Harpies don't. They've often overstepped the bounds of stylist and client, putting their hands on him in inappropriate ways.

"Want me to talk to them?"

"Nah, I can handle 'em." Giving my shoulder a squeeze, he saunters off, whistling Hard Day's Night.

Sex, money, power. Three intoxicating things that drive us all, Un, En, or other.

Chapter 4

Where Rey's night is a storm, mine's a breeze, nothing but blowouts, roller sets, and cuts. At least in the world of hair it's a breeze, interaction with coworkers is another story. Tucking the last roller into place on Mrs. Nelson, I replace the heavy plastic cape with a lighter silky one and motion her toward the dryers. Dara's hands pause and shoulders hunch, her posture becoming rigid until we pass. It's been over two weeks since I took the job and she still hasn't come to terms with me being The Shadow.

After setting the dryer and pulling down the hood, I make a point of circling well away from her as I hightail it to the break room. Silly, I know, but her rejection hurts more than chopping the knuckle off your finger with a pair of dull shears. Trust me, I've done it and it ain't pretty. Dara and I've been friends since beauty school, a friendship I question since learning I've been on her goddess, Sekhmet's radar. Was it really friendship or just following orders? I'd recently learned she was sent to watch over me and kill me if I stepped out of line. A line I've crossed many times in recent history.

From what I've gathered, I'm a true necromancer. I can control the dead, or in Dara's case the undead. Not exactly a Talent vampires encourage. The usual course of actions is to hunt necromancers down and annihilate them. Strangely, I've been given a reprieve. Is this reprieve because she really does care, or are we dealing with more divine politics? No offense to Sekhmet, I appreciate her helping to heal me after my Collector adventure, but I'm sick of gods playing me.

I'm also sick of doubt. Doubting who and what I am. Seriously, what the hel is a schattenkind? Am I really a necromancer? Doubting my relationships and if they're because of who and what I am. Almost everyone in my life seems to be connected to what I am. Doubting if I can handle what I am. Am I strong enough not to resist the power I feel when I use my shadowy Talents? According to everyone, Vereinen wasn't. He was driven mad and banished because of he couldn't resist the heady power of using his Talent.

Crazy or not, finding Einen would put me at an advantage. What I grew to believe a childhood manifestation had come to life, cruelly yanked away again before I could find out what I need to know. Only another—the only other—shadow child can teach me how to use these Talents and how to survive as his replacement as Shadow.

Finding him was in the top five of why I took

the position of Shadow. Not because I wanted to rekindle the relationship from childhood, or because he's incredibly hot—it doesn't hurt, but I'm surrounded by sexy men—but because of his knowledge. With the collar gone—another reason on that top five list, nothing worse than a necklace that kills if you use your Talents, even if I do deserve it—figuring out where Var and Vana stashed him should be easier. Not easy, but easier. All I need is a starting point. I can give border hopping a try without the collar. If I can hop my way back to where we used to meet, I might find a clue. Too bad I have no idea how I did it in the past.

I pop the top on a can of Dr. Pepper and let the sweet bubbles tickle their way across my tongue. If only the momentary bliss of those bubbles could tickle away all my doubts and fears.

The door swings open and Win peeks around the corner. "Keely?"

Winola Mallory is the newest addition to the Fey Creations family. The wind sprite had been contracted by Var Royd as a temporary receptionist. I hated that he'd interfered, but I was desperate to fill the position.

Our receptionist, Jenny Abbot, fell under the spell of love, lust… hel, I don't know what it was that attracted her to Stanley Lewis, better known as The Collector. Maybe because they were both anomalies, Unchants born of two Enchants. It's rare that a child of two Ens is born without Talents, but it happens. The two of them had stolen hair clippings that Stanley cremated and compressed into gems. Those gems were placed in an amulet and used to control Ens and take their Talents. The amulet was lost during my struggle with The Collector, a niggling fact that haunts me. Out of guilt, fear, or loyalty to me, Jenny turned on him and he killed her. Of course he planned to resurrect that love by taking my Talents, but I killed him, turning the very Talent he wanted against him. I called his victims and let them get their revenge.

With all the bad press and rumors, not a single candidate jumped to fill the receptionist position. Can't blame anyone for not wanting to work surrounded by so much uncertainty and possible danger. Besides, Win fit the bill of what we needed, she's efficient, organized, and it doesn't hurt that she's Nyssa's friend. Sprites, whether air, water, fire, or earth, seem to flock together. Nyssa vouching for her doesn't totally ease my mind as to where her loyalties lie, but it helps.

"Yeah?"

"Have you got time for a cut while your client is under the dryer?"

"Cut and style or just a cut?"

"Men's cut, looks pretty basic to me and he asked for you."

"Did you recognize him at all?"

"No, but he's kind of cute. In a geeky, bookish sort of way."

I glance at the clock, plenty of time and cutting hair beats sitting back here worrying over things I can't do anything about right now. "Yeah, I've got time, be right out."

Chapter 5

Tweed slacks peek out from under the cape covering the body Nyssa's bent over at the shampoo bowl. Could it be the guy from the skywalk? Nah, has to be a coincidence. Still tweed, in August, in Iowa… Win had said geeky and bookish. Between the struggle of Nyssa's towel drying and the fumbling attempts to get his glasses on, I can't see his face clear enough to—well, shit, it is Mr. Skywalk. The simple explanation spanning the gap from bumping into him to him making an appointment is a coincidence, right? Coincidences that aren't coincidences are becoming the norm lately. Can you blame me for questioning every little thing?

His smile stretches ear to ear as he approaches my chair. "Miss Fey, thank you for making room for me in your schedule on such short notice."

"I had an opening and you filled it, Mr. …"

He places his glasses on my vanity. "Mortonson, but please call me Mort."

Back to the mirror, amusement twinkling in violet eyes, Nyssa hands me a clean towel.

"Thanks, Nys, will you check on Mrs. Nelson?"

She teeters off on three inch heels, shoulders

shaking in silent laughter. Something about Mort has tripped her funny bone. Probably his fashion choices. Like she's got room to talk with her penchant for 60s bouffant teasing, heavy liner and lashes. A look she's sported since supposedly dating the King of Rock and Roll. Rumors I can't confirm, having been born after his marriage to his Unchant wife. Yes, Elvis is an Enchant and no, he's not dead. As Tommy Lee Jones put it, he just went home.

"How would you like your hair cut, Mort?"

Running his fingers through the tousled, blond spikes, he leans forward in the chair, pushing it into some semblance of his usual style. I grab the back of his cape as he sits, guiding it over the chair as he leans back.

"Can you shape it up? It's a bit long over the ears and collar."

Nodding, I grab a comb and begin sectioning. Tipping the ends all over, his hair is already so short a wonder cut is all that's needed. Wonder as in wonder if I cut anything.

"So what brings you to The Meadows and my salon in particular, Mort?"

"I needed a haircut and heard your talents praised."

Prickles of warning crawl across my skin and I clamp down on my shields. The last thing I need is my Talents rising over a word. He could very well mean my talent as a stylist, not the other Talent.

He shrugs and I pull my shears away from his ear. "So I thought I'd stop and see if you had room in your schedule."

Once he settles, I comb the fraction of growth over his ear before settling my shears against the point where ear meets face. "I just find it… strange."

"Strange?" He twists in the chair and I again pull back my hand, grabbing his shoulders, righting him. I can work around movement, but prefer my clients sit still and understand why they can't move around. This is why I have a ban on the twelve and under crowd when it comes to my appointments. Dealing with fidgeting children is bad, but when you add in parents who think their darlings can do no wrong, it becomes a nightmare. It's just easier to have a no child policy.

"Do that again and you might lose an ear."

"Sorry."

"Don't be sorry, just hold still. I'm holding shears, very sharp shears. It's not your first haircut."

"True."

"You don't find it at all strange?"

"I didn't recognize you earlier."

Head tipped down as I work around the perimeter, I look him in the eye using the mirror. "Okay, call me suspicious, but I'm not buying it."

"It was just a freak accident."

"Still not buying it, tell me the truth."

He sighs. "Fine, I knew who you were and took a chance on where you'd be today."

This time I take a step back, not because of his movement, but the shaking of my hands. "So you're following me?"

"Following isn't quite the word to describe it."

"Then what word would you use?" "Educated estimates of your locations." He gulps as I stare him down in the mirror. I need to get him out of here and fast, before I lose control and something bad happens. Something that could put me out of business permanently and back in the Enchant Containment Unit with a collar around my neck. I see Dara staring in my peripheral and I lean down to continue the work around his ear. "Quickly, tell me why you're making *educated estimates of my locations?*"

"My family has studied your kind for some time now. Of course none of them were as lucky as I am. I actually get to meet one of you in the flesh."

Huh? Studied my *kind?* His announcement is creepy and rude on so many levels. I feel violated. Dirty. Yet, I want to know more, but this is not the place for such a sensitive discussion. I'll need a more private, but still public—I have no idea if Mort is friend or foe—to delve deeper into what he knows. Unable to look into the eyes of a kid on his first trip to Disney Land, I grab my trimmer and flip the switch. Taking a breath, I hold it, mulling over how to respond as the tiny vibrating blades shave way the peach fuzz on his neck.

"I've upset you. If you have a moment, I can—"

"Not the place or time, Mort." I slip the clippers back into their slot.

"I apologize, but I think I can help—

"I said, drop it. I don't want to discuss it at work."

Grabbing the dryer, I almost feel bad seeing his dejected expression in the mirror. Almost. Part of me wants to believe he wants to help me, but if he can't keep his mouth shut in public, nothing he says or does is going to help. I also question who else he has, or will, spill his research to. Slow burning heat of instinctual fear builds in my gut.

Clicking off the dryer, I slowly put it back in its holder and turn to face him. "Have you talked to anyone else about me or your findings?"

Adam's apple bobbing, eyes flicking from side to side, hands fidgeting under the cape, he opens his mouth, but nothing comes out.

"Who have you talked to, Mort?"

"Well, she *is* the reason I found you."

The telltale signs of tightness in my skin and a growing need to itch every part of it signals I'm pushing my limits of control. "Who, Mort?"

His eyes bulge as he grasps and pulls at the front of the cape. "Please—can't breathe."

Ashamed, I loosen my grip on the back of the cape and take a quick glance to see if anyone noticed me trying to choke my client. Talk about bad for business. Hel's Realm, she may not be looking directly at me, but I know Dara saw everything. Probably heard a good chunk of what was discussed around the blow-dry time too. Bet it's been added to the list of reasons to finish me. Oh, well, I'll worry about that later.

Taking off the cape, I place my hands on Mort's shoulders, pushing him down into the chair he's trying to escape from. Guess my status has changed from fascinating to scary. "Who did you talk to, Mort?"

"Nastasia Athory."

Chapter 6

A collective sigh follows the chime of the bell, signaling the departure of the client of the night. Win races to flip the lock and the stereo booms to levels closer to the local night club, Atramentous, than a hair salon. My light breeze of a night is turning out to be a tornado. A swirl of elation, anger, and fear, with a surly coworker in its eye.

The business card Mort so carefully wrapped in the tip he forced into my hand burns a hole in my pocket. All I want to do is go upstairs and Google him, but leaving now would raise too many eyebrows. Why did he have to mention Stasia Athory? What kind of nightmare maze am I stuck in that always leads back to her?

As the others turn cleaning into a party, Dara stands polishing her shears. Methodically opening and closing the blades, wiping them each time with a slowness bordering on psycho. I don't want to be in her head right now, because more than likely I'm on her mind.

We've both kept secrets from the other, but I blame that on the gods. She chose her path and I'd been forced to choose, but in the end we are pieces on a game board, used by the higher-ups for their amusements and agendas. Beyond that, I know we were—are—friends, or she would've followed Sekhmet's orders and taken me out when she learned I'd joined the ranks of Royd. There's always a chance that Sekhmet, like Hel, finds this union useful in her bigger picture. Who can say how the gods think, they're always ten steps ahead of the rest of us.

Weeks of tension between Dara and me is taking a toll on everything it touches. I'm tired of playing cat and mouse. Time to find out if we're friends, frenemies, or full-on enemies. I toss a towel toward my vanity, sending containers of product skittering and rolling across the surface and onto the floor.

Gyrating coworkers freeze, giving the appearance of a dance floor museum, and the sing-along stutters to a stop. There's a wild, trapped animal look in Rey's eyes as he pushes Win toward the vacuum. He grabs Nyssa's hand and tugs. When she won't move, he practically picks her up, and follows Win toward reception. Dara doesn't bother pausing polishing her shears, or looking up. The only indication she noticed my tantrum is the slight tightening of her shoulders.

Anger and frustration driving me, I wrench the cloth from her hands and toss it, causing another avalanche of product bottles to fall from her vanity.

"Enough, we're going to talk this out."

One brow raises, hiding behind her bangs.

"Now." I grab her arm and attempt to pull her toward the break room. It's difficult to move a rock, but when the rock pulls back you end up teetering on your heels. This isn't the first time I've neglected to remember Dara's vampire strength. Hel, it's not the first time I've forgotten she's a vamp. Friendship will do that.

Managing to right myself thanks to my grip on her arm, I turn and look at her. Fangs bared, not a good sign. Then I make the mistake of looking her in the eye, molten gold swirls hypnotically.

"Don't try your vamp tricks on me." Centering my gaze on the downward point of her heart shaped bangs to keep from falling under, I stand my ground. "We can't go on like this. We need to talk it out. It's not good for business—"

"Then consider this my two weeks."

"—and it's horrible for our friendship." I should have known she'd say something so stupidly childish. I let go of her arm and point toward the back room. "Not accepted, now get your ass in the break room."

Her head tilts to one side, and her usually smooth, emotionless face crinkles in confusion.

"Now!" Unholy shit, when did I become so ballsy? Could it be I'm coming to terms with being one of the monsters under the bed? I spin on my heels and march off before the quaking in my gut radiates outward to my whole body. Show no weakness. It will ruin the moment, not to mention feed her predatory instinct and I really don't want to be what's for dinner.

I stand to the side of the doorway and motion her inside. It's pretty obvious she doesn't like it, but she rounds the table and sits.

Grabbing a Pepper, I take a seat across from her. Yeah, I sounded and acted authoritative and she seems okay with it, but why take chances? Safer to keep the table between us, for now.

"I know you're pissed off at me."

Her lips twist as if I forced her to taste something hidden in the back of the fridge. "It was bad enough when you were dating him, now—"

"I wasn't dating him, it was just dinner." My lips might be moving, but she doesn't skip a beat.

"—you are working for him."

"Dara, please, we've discussed this. You know why I took the job."

"It does not mean I agree with your decision."

"Hel's Realm, my choices where slim and none." I hold up my hands weighing each option. "Spending the rest of my life in the CU, or take the job? Tormented by the Blood Countess's daughter, or take the job? Becoming a minion of the dark goddess, or take the job?"

A shiver runs up my back. I'd pretty much

attained minion status with the favor I owe. Now, I've unwittingly cemented it with taking the job, but it's not the time or place to bring that up. Hel, there probably won't ever be a time or place to gracefully divulge that little secret.

"You did not need to become his servant, I would have protected you from those threats and more."

And more, those words, or maybe it's her tone, strike fear deep within. She's part of that *and more* with her mission to watch over me and *take me out* if I step out of line. I know I've inched closer to that line in the past than either of us want, but have I crossed it by taking the job?

"Look, Dara, I know the strain this puts you under, but there was no other way. I needed my Talents back and you couldn't do that, any more than you can promise to protect me twenty-four-seven. Even you have… limitations."

Leaning forward, elbows on knees, she's hunched over so I can't see her face, making it damn near impossible to get even the slightest read on what she's thinking. Not that it's easy when I can see her face, she's a master at keeping her emotions hidden when needed.

"Stupid question, but I've got to ask anyway, does your goddess know?"

The slight movement of her head causes a cold sweat to rise across my skin. Licking my lips,

I choke out the next question. "Did she tell you to… pull the trigger?"

A rush of relief escapes from between my lips when she shakes her head. I wonder why she didn't give the kill order, but I'm not stupid enough to put the question into words. I'm sure she has her reasons, just like every other god I've been dealing with lately. Some sort of end game that includes me working with Var Royd.

"Where does this leave us?"

Dara slowly lifts her head and I meet her gaze, a show of trust that she won't try and mind fuck me. Truthfully, I wonder if her vamp tricks will work on me. If she did try, fear would be an instant response and it's an involuntary trigger for my Talents. I've already proven certain aspects of my Talents can control her. This is not something I want to test, especially when I'm trying to heal the rift between us, and keep Sekhmet from ordering my execution.

"Just because I took the job doesn't mean we can't be friends. Can we call a truce?"

She sighs, straightening up in her chair. One corner of her mouth turning upward and she nods. "I have missed movie night."

"Me too."

"Just do me the favor of not putting yourself in a position where I cannot help you." She gives my shoulder a squeeze before leaving me to ponder

if that means a position where Sekhmet screams
for my head.

Chapter 7

CC sits on the window seat, staring down the lone mourning dove perched on the sill. He's hissed, slapped the screen, growled and even screeched, but it won't leave. Luckily, he hasn't tried a full-on attack, I can't even think about the consequences of my cat plummeting two stories to the sidewalk below. No matter how *special* I think he is, I don't think he'd survive the impact.

Leaning down, I look the bird in the eyes. "Tell Hel, I'll contact her when I'm ready. My dance card is full right now."

The bird coos and bobs its head, but still doesn't leave.

"You better shoo before Teiran and Ric get here. I can't guarantee your safety." As the words leave my lips, a leather clad, vampire elf on a sleek, oxblood Valkyrie pulls up below. "Seriously, hit the air, Teiran can't be far behind and we know how he feels about your kind and your mistress."

It cocks its head to one side and blinks. Great, that's all I need a bird who is playing dumb blonde. I don't have time to find out which it is, Ric is on his way up. Running to the bathroom, I grab a spray bottle of water. This should get it moving. Entering the living room I take aim, but my visitor knocks and the bird flies off before I can pull the trigger. Damn bird.

"Come on in."

The door swings open and I bite my lower lip. Gods, he looks good. Golden beauty showcased in black. I've never been envious of a coat before, but damn, I'd like to trade places with his right now.

His lips curl upward in a seductively teasing smile. "You do know that only works on witches."

"What? Oh, I was using this to chase CC off the counter." I quickly set the water bottle on the table next to the couch. Glancing at the narrow eyed cat, I grimace, hoping he understands the little white lie.

Ric takes off the jacket, draping it carefully across the back of a chair. "Teiran should be here shortly. Should we start without him?"

"Uh-huh." I'm too busy checking out the black, painted-on jeans and teeshirt to pay attention to the words coming out of his mouth.

"Then I suggest you strip and sit in the middle of the floor."

"Okay."

A deep belly laugh fills the air, jerking me back from my inner debate over boxers, briefs, or commando under that denim.

"Wait, what did you say?"

"Never mind." Ric shakes his head, grinning.

He reaches into his front pocket, an amazing feat considering how tight they are—most definitely commando, no lines. Moving toward me, he holds out his hand, fingers uncurling to reveal the moonstone charm he'd given me for my birthday. It used to hang on the collar. I'd been so elated at having it removed, I'd forgotten the stone. Shitty of me, I know, but there had been more important things on my mind.

"I thought you might like this back."

His tone is soft along with his features, and his eyes hold something I don't think I want to see. Lust I can handle, but this looks like something more. In a perfect world I could see myself falling for him, hard, but my world is far from perfect right now. Hel, we barely know each other and I can't deal with that kind of thing right now. Here's hoping I'm reading him wrong, but just in case, I carefully take the charm from his palm, trying to avoid any skin on skin contact. No more distractions, no complications, right?

"Thank you, I'd wondered where it had gone. I'll just put it in the bedroom before it gets lost. Help yourself to anything in the fridge if you're thirsty."

He nods, heading toward the kitchen as I dash down the hall to my bedroom. I don't own a lot of jewelry, but what I have is scattered on the chest of drawers, or tossed in a box. Precious and semi-precious stones deserve more care than the shoe box I use to store my cheap, costume stuff.

I search the room for a suitable resting place for my one good piece of jewelry, but nothing strikes me as an appropriate spot. The opening creak of the front door and muffled voices make my decision for me. I lift the lid of a miniature grand piano given to me by my high school music teacher at graduation. This should do the trick, as long as I don't forget I put it here. A very real possibility, but the least of my worries at present. I've got two over achieving, alpha-males waiting for me in the other room.

"Neither of us are qualified to do what is asked of us."

Hearing Teiran's frustration, I hesitate halfway down the hall, what's a little eavesdropping hurt?

"I know, but we do not have a choice. It is what Lord Royd asked of us, besides, there is no one else. We will have to do our best to guide her."

Good, they're as confused about this as I am. Tiptoeing backward, I shut my bedroom door with a little extra force and head out into the living room. "Hi, Teiran, didn't hear you come in. Are those for me?" I point to the bouquet of flowers held haphazardly at his side. "You shouldn't have."

He scowls, thrusting them toward me. "I did nothing, but deliver."

There was never a doubt in my mind of the unlikelihood of him giving me flowers. If he ever did, I doubt they would be roses. Only one person sends me roses and the scrawling handwriting on the card confirms they are from Var. *Forgive me.* Yay, another "forgive me" to add to the pile. My own scowl matches Teiran's as I toss them on the kitchen table. Too bad he's so full of himself he can't say the words to my face, it would go a lot further in the forgiveness category if he did.

When I turn around there's a hint of a smile on Ric's face and while Teiran's scowl hasn't turned upside-down, it's less intense. Must have earned some brownie points for not fawning over Royd's roses. It shouldn't matter what they think, but it does. We are partners. And they're even prettier when they aren't pissy. Like any girl, I like pretty things. Pretty, delectable things. So pretty it makes you wanna rip—Ric's smile wides and the burning heat moves from my lower regions to my cheeks. Damn it! He better not be digging around in my head.

I am not "digging around in your head", you are projecting your thoughts loud and clear. Even Teiran can sense what you are thinking.

Sure enough, there's a dangerous light in Teiran's sapphire eyes. Crap, crap, crap! *So you can read minds.*

As I have explained, when you project your

thoughts toward me, otherwise I only sense bits and pieces, or emotions. Teiran, on the other hand should not be able to sense what you are thinking, it is probably the change in your pheromones.

Hel's Realm, he can smell my emotions?

Yes, although, your joint connection through Hel might be playing a part in what he senses…

Slamming a couple extra bricks into my mental walls, I stalk off to the kitchen, grab a glass and let the water run until it's cold. I have the urge to stick my head under the faucet, but settle for gulping down a glass full before turning around again.

Somehow, I manage to keep forgetting Ric's ability to "sense" thoughts and emotions. I also conveniently forget about Teiran being Hel's hound.

Ric clears his throat. "Perhaps we should get started with your training, Keely."

"Yeah," I sigh and set the glass down. "The sooner we start the sooner it's over."

Chapter 8

"Relax, find your center." By the fourth hour of me trying to "find my center"—whatever the hel that means—Ric's patience is stretched as far as mine, he's just better at hiding it.

"How can I relax with the Big Bad Wolf over there huffing and puffing?"

"I am not a wolf, woman." I don't need to see him to know Teiran's shooting eye-daggers in my direction.

"Whatever, point is, your attitude is anything but conducive to *finding my center*." I unwind from my cross-legged position on the floor. I'd probably do better practicing on my own, but there's always the danger it will get out of hand and I'll need help to rein it in. Teiran's Talent with darkness has proven useful in such cases. Then again, if I was alone, I could check out Mort Mortonson. Maybe he has a clue about how my Talents work. All I have to do is get them to leave.

Ric holds out a hand to help me to my feet. "I suggest we take a break from your training."

"Ya think?" The tension in the room is enough to make me want to spill every dog reference I'd heard Dara use on Teiran, instead I settle for a glare in his direction.

"Yes, I think."

As pretty as Ric's smile is, it does nothing to improve my mood, nor do the three quick raps against the door. So much for trying to trick them into leaving. Ric, Teiran, Rey and Nyssa have magical codes to get past the wards to my private space that alert me when they arrive. Anyone else needs to be buzzed in. Days like this I'm tempted to revoke or change Teiran's code and not tell him. There's only one other person with free rein over the building and her entrance is going to be like lighting a match to super-hold hairspray.

"Come on in, Dara."

Even in cutoffs and an old hair-color splattered shirt, the woman looks like she belongs in a fashion spread. A dark, exotic counter image to my beyond-pale averageness. Envy thy name is Keely.

"Perfect timing, First Arrow." Ric dips his head in respect and Dara follows suit.

"Sword." She turns assessing Teiran, his perpetual frown deeper than usual, and raises a brow. "Shield."

"Arrow."

Looks like I won't have to search out a fire extinguisher after all, everyone seems to be on fairly neutral terms. Does this have anything to do with our chat last night? Makes a girl suspicious, and what is she in *perfect* time for? Why do I get the feeling I'm in for more torture?

"Why do I get the feeling this is a setup?"

"Setup? Miss Kanika has graciously offered to help in the next step of your training. We all felt you would be more comfortable with another woman present."

I stare at Ric, fighting to keep my jaw from hitting the floor. "More comfortable with another woman present? What the hel kind of kinky-ass-training needs another woman present?"

He laughs. Hel, even Teiran laughs. Dara just smirks at me and shakes her head. "Get your mind out of the gutter, I am here to help with physical training."

"Again, what the h—"

She spins me around, twisting my arm behind my back until I buckle at the knees. Her other hand tangles in my hair, pulling my head to the side, exposing my neck. "Physical training."

I swallow, fear threatens to pound its way out of my chest. "So the three of you are going to take turns beating me up?"

"Do not be flippant, we are going to teach how *not* to get beat up."

Her breath against my neck sends a flutter of terror through my stomach, followed by another when I see Ric staring at my throat. Yes, he's gentlemanly and sweet, but he's still a vampire.

I don't even want to know what's going through Teiran's mind and I'm glad I can't see him from my painfully precarious position.

At least Ric has the decency to look embarrassed when he notices me watching him. Clearing his throat he looks at anything but me. "Perhaps we should use the term self-defense, instead of physical training."

"Either way, I think you've proven your point, I suck at defending myself. Dara, can you let me go?"

Her grip loosens and I stagger away, rubbing my arm.

"We are here to remedy that problem." Teiran stands in front of me, arms crossed over his chest, eyes assessing me like he's at a livestock sale.

"Is this another of Var's orders?"

Teiran lifts his head, distain gleaming from under hooded lids. "No, it is the consensus of the group that you need to learn to defend yourself."

"Look guys, I appreciate your concern, but the first rule of defense is not to put yourself in a situation where you need to defend yourself. And if you find yourself in such a situation, put as much distance between you and your would-be attacker as possible. Flight, not fight, that's my position on self-defense, and I'm sticking to it."

"Then you have not been sticking to your position. You have done nothing but put yourself in harm's way, time and time again." The condescension so apparent in Teiran's expression now drips from his words.

"Have not."

"Teiran is correct, Keely, whether you mean to, or not, you have placed yourself in danger more than once since we've known you."

I expect the looks and none too subtle noises expressing their disdain from Teiran and even Dara, but not from Ric. I kind of figured he'd agree with me.

"Not fair, Ric." I'm feeling a little more than bitter now. "I didn't have any of these problems before I met you two. Maybe it's because of your interference in my life that it keeps happening."

Ric shakes his head in a gradual descent. "We both know that is not the case. The emergence of your Talents is what brought you to our attention."

"I can't help it. The Sisters put a block on them and their block began to deteriorate when you two showed up. They were trying to protect me from your boss."

With a long exaggerated breath of irritation, Dara steps between us. "This discussion is futile, what is done, is done and now you must move on. Self-defense is indispensable. Even if you had not taken the job of Shadow, I would have urged you to learn to defend yourself."

I find it curious, the woman tasked with making sure I don't become a threat, wants me to learn to defend myself. Do her warrior sensibilities find it easier, or more honorable, to kill someone who can fight back? Whatever the case, Dara's right, there is no way I'm going to win this discussion.

"Fine, what do I have to do?"

Her lips slowly curve upward and her eyes flash with delight. "First you must chose a weapon."

Chapter 9

"You can't be serious, the closest I've come to using a weapon is a kitchen knife and that was against hapless veggies." They're circled around me, a trio of crossed arms and parental, take-no-shit expressions. This is not going as expected. What am I saying? This kind of thing is exactly what I should expect, them lording their centuries of experience over me.

"Now that you have taken the position of Shadow it is imperative you know how to defend yourself." Teiran's expression is grim, as usual, but I pick up on the hint he's trying to come to terms with working with me.

"What? Having the ability to control killer shadows, or having the dead do my bidding isn't enough?"

"No, it is not enough. Your control over your Talents is… unreliable. None of us are qualified to train you in their use, but we are more than qualified to teach you to use a blade." Ric's sword appears as if a magical extension of his hand. Someday, I'm going to have to ask him where he hides the damn thing.

Already looming over me, Teiran's perfect posture seems to broaden menacingly and I take a step back. All he needs to do is sprout claws and my flight reflex will over whelm common sense. "Your own body."

"Or a firearm." A tiny gun lays in the palm of Dara's hand. She conceals more weapons than a body has a right. She's a freaking, walking arsenal in Daisy Dukes and a tee. Makes a girl wonder how she'd deal with airline travel, if that's even possible with her daylight affliction.

I turn in sequence as each lists a possible weapon. All of which I am totally unfamiliar with, well, besides my body and let's just say using it as a weapon is laughable at best. I'm a runner, not a fighter.

"Look, I know you all have my best interests at heart, but none of the above is feasible. I don't have your strength or centuries of training."

Facing Ric, I grimace and shake my head. "You have an advantage in the concealment game, I can't pass a sword off as a fashion accessory. On top of that, there are major doubts that I could even lift one, let alone use one."

"As for using my body,"—I turn on Teiran, his eyes following the motion of my hand down my slender frame with the tiniest bit of heat—"I'm hardly intimidating and don't have the extra added bonus of sprouting claws at a moment's notice."

"Firearms, even one as cute as that one, aren't always an option either. We all know they don't work on everything that might threaten me, or mine. And again, all of these weapons take years of practice to be proficient enough to use them. Years I don't have to spare. If you all insist I use a weapon other than my Talent, I need something I can learn quickly and be slightly efficient with. Something that will be a detriment to an attacker, not the attack-ee."

Dara lowers her hand, palming the tiny pistol.

Teiran clasps his hands behind his back. "She will still need to learn the art of hand-to-hand."

There doesn't seem to be any budging him on this subject, not that the idea of wrestling around on the floor with him is wholly unpleasant.

"Agreed," adds Ric, his sword disappearing to wherever it goes when not in use.

Maybe learning a little self-defense has some perks, like two hot guys wanting to get physical with me. Heat rises in my cheeks and I have to look away. It might also be a detriment.

"She needs a weapon she is comfortable with, something small enough to conceal and easily wielded." Dara lowers herself into a chair, contemplating the options. "An item no one would think twice about her carrying."

Teiran takes up residence on the couch, while Ric paces the expanse of the living room.

This could take hours, so we might as well get comfortable. The bottle of red on the kitchen counter is calling my name, but I figure it's in bad taste to mix alcohol and weapons chatter. "Coffee, anyone?"

Three heads bob in varying degrees. I take it as a sign of agreement and head off to start the machine.

Me? Carry a weapon? What a joke. Would be attackers rejoice, I'm more likely to do their job for them. Maybe I'd get lucky and brand them with a curling iron. A straight-edge is a possibility, I suppose, but the thought of slitting someone's throat sends a shiver from the top of my head to the bottoms of my feet. No, I don't think I could do it, better to let the pros handle any possible skirmishes. My best weapons are gathered in the next room. Think I'll take a page out of Var's rule book and use the tools I've been given.

A coffee mug nearly bites it as the silence behind me breaks with a flurry of activity. Heart trying to beat its way out of my chest, I clutch the countertop, not wanting to turn around and see a fight has broken out in my absence. Gods only know what will happen when you put these three together.

When my pulse returns to normal, I turn and face the trio huddled by my shelves. Ric is reaching for something very dear to me.

"Hey, careful with those, they're an antique."

Gingerly, he lifts my prized possession from its display stand. Before I can cross the room to stop him, he pulls the shears from their sheath. "I think we have found a weapon she will be comfortable wielding. One no one will question."

"Those are an antique, meant for display, not a weapon for backstreet brawls." I attempt to snatch the shears from Ric, but they end up in Teiran's hands.

"On the contrary, they are hardly an antique,"— he slides them from the sheath, testing both the inside and outside edges along his thumb—"but very much a weapon. One that can be used as both shears and dagger." He slips them back into their protective metal sheath and hands them over to me.

"How dare you insinuate they aren't real. The Sisters gave them to me as a graduation present from beauty school and told me they were fourteenth century bodice shears." I cradle them close to my chest, unwilling to believe they are a fake.

"My dear, Keely, I insinuate nothing. Whatever you were led to believe, your shears are replicas. The original pair are in a private collection, if I recall correctly."

Wonderful, another lie by The Sisters. A small one, yes, but when you add them all up it doesn't matter how big or small. There is always the possibility I misheard them since it was a pretty exciting day for an eighteen year old Keely. The pristine condition of the shears and their sheath should have been a clue, no antique is that shiny and clean. My heart sinks as light dances against tiny red stones I once believed were rubies decorating the ornate cross-guard and sheath. It just didn't dawn on me to question them. Either way, finding out my precious bodice shears are a replica is a bit of a let down. But a bigger problem is my teachers expect me to use them. And not to cut hair.

Chapter 10

August's heat is visible in blurred waves radiating from the pavement and the sweat coated, reddened skin of bikers and hikers. My iced white chocolate is losing its cool, becoming a diluted version of itself. Watered-down or not, I'm finishing it. It's still coffee.

The heat doesn't bother me, it's the humidity that's killing me. Thick enough it feels more like swimming—not that I have a lot of experience with swimming, more like drowning—than walking. And let's not get into what it does to my hair. Thankfully, ponytails and buns are all the rage on the Trail, right along with the haute couture of denim cutoffs and baggy tees.

It's not a terribly long walk to the bridge, but long enough to make me wish I'd worn tennies instead of my trusty old sandals. Fine for running errands, but not meant for long, purposeful treks. Too bad I don't know if Mort can actually help me, which might justify the growing ache of my feet.

My heart flutters as I reach the edge of my destination. Why the hel did I ever agree to meet him here? Before the High Trestle Trail was constructed, this section was often referred to as Iowa's Stonehenge. Twenty-two concrete pillars that refused to move, supporting the memory of a bridge crossing the river valley. Many claim there is some sort of magical gateway located under the bridge near the center. I've never witnessed this phenomenon, but that's not really surprising since I don't make a habit of hanging out thirteen stories above a body of water.

I'm not afraid of heights, I'm afraid of falling. And oh, yeah, drowning. The river is shallower through here, but after my last unintentional dip in the river, I have no desire to test the water levels. Another forced swimming lesson is not high on my list of things to do today, or anytime in the future.

The breeze of bikers and nasty rumblings of power walkers skirting around me pushes me closer to the edge than desired.

"Get over it, Keely, you can't stand in the middle of the road and expect people not to be upset." I white knuckle the rail, refusing to look down. Instead I take in the leafy greens and blue and white of the horizon, my stomach rolling and head becoming light and airy.

A shadow stretches out beside me, along with a scent that triggers memories of high school boys who bathed in a cologne with a name that escapes me now. I faintly remember a jockey, or some other horse symbol on a green bottle.

I turn and face a young man, maybe half my age, clad in tweed. He should be sweltering in this heat, but shows no sign, not even a sheen on his fair skin. His hair is a perfect blond helmet and pale blue eyes shine with glee behind horn rimmed glasses.

"Thank you for agreeing to meet with me, Miss Fey."

"Let's cut to the chase, what do you want, Mr. Mortonson?" Call me gun-shy, but experience proves those who want to meet me usually want *something*. Like to kill me, use my Talents, or drain my blood. For all I know, this crackpot wants all of the above.

"Please, call me Mort, all my friends do."

"What is it you want, Mort?"

He smiles shyly, dragging a toe across the ground. "You are the only one of your kind walking this earth, the only *accessible* schattenkind."

"We've already established this. What do you want?"

"As I've said, my family has studied your kind…" He gazes out over the water. "It's really quite beautiful, isn't it?"

I sigh and shake my head. "I'm not going to ask you again, Mort. Just tell me what you want."

His brilliant smile highlights my stupidity in using his nickname. "I want to help you. As I said—"

I rotate my hand over and over. "Your family has studied my kind, get on with it."

"It goes back to my great-grandfather's time. During World War II, he was part of a group called the Ahnenerbe—"

"The on a what?"

"On-en-air-bo—"

I dismiss his pronunciation with a wave of my hand. "Just tell me what it is and be quick about it, I don't have all day."

"It was—still is—a group that studies the anthropological and cultural history of the German race. My great-grandfather's job was to collect information of an occult nature for the Nazi—"

"Whoa, hold it right there, I don't need to hear any more. You can goose-step your tweed-wearing-Neo-Nazi ass right on out of here."

"Miss Fey, I am not a Nazi, Neo or otherwise."

"You just said, your grandfather worked for the Nazis—"

"My *great*-grandfather—"

"Whatever, don't care, want nothing to do with anything pertaining to or related to the Nazi party. Including you and your *great*-grandfather."

I turn and he grabs my arm. "Miss Fey, wait—"

"Hands off."

His grip loosens, hand sliding away. Eyes wide, he swallows. The stench of fear emanating from him tells me I'm stepping into dangerous territory.

"So it is true." Head tipped forward, he peers over thick frames, staring into my eyes.

"What?"

"Your eyes, they are like an abyss when your powers rise. Fascinating." One finger slides his glasses along the bridge of his nose. His eyes shine bright enough to light up downtown.

"Fascinating? I could kill you at any moment and you just stand there and say, fascinating? You claimed to know all about me and my kind."

"Yes, fascinating. I only know what has been documented about the other schattenkind. Seeing one in the flesh goes beyond my wildest dreams."

Great, I'm a Nazi wet dream. I know I should walk away, but my curiosity is piqued. What does he know about me and my *kind*? Can I get my hands on this documentation? Will it be of any use, or merely speculation and crap I already know? "What exactly do you have documented?"

His thin frame trembles, barely containing the excitement of being asked. I have to dodge the exaggerated hand movements or risk being knocked down. "Everything we could find. Of course, none of it's first hand, not being able to study the subject one-on-one. But all accounts are from those who had contact with him and were willing to talk."

"In other words, hearsay."

He shakes his head, totally believing his own

BS. "No, no, these Enchants *knew* the other schattenkind."

Yeah, right, I know how tight-lipped the En community is when it comes to Vereinen. "And you have proof, how?"

"One subject actually worked side by side with him."

I can't control it, my jaw drops. "And who was this?"

"Why your own co-worker, Alric Brand, of course."

There is no fucking way Ric would have blasted super-secret Var Royd business to the Nazis. I don't buy it, but then again, there was a conversation outside my bedroom door, between Var and Ric, after I came home from the CU. Something about Var's wife and Nazis. *The Nazis made you what you are.* Is that how they gleaned their info about Einen? Tortured him, sucked any info they could out of him, then changed him? This would explain why he's so cautious, almost haunted when I question him about his past and Einen.

Mort jumps back as a flurry of winged, pale grey bodies come between us. Some take up residence on the railing others harmlessly land at our feet, it's the one perched on my shoulder that sends a chill down my spine. One empty socket and one perfect crystal blue eye, stare at me from the mourning dove's face.

Shit. Why is it when things start to fall in my favor, I get tossed to the pavement?

Chapter 11

Hel's freaky-deaky eyes, or should I say eye and empty socket, stare at me from her feathered minion. At least it's only her *eyes* the bird sports, having to look at a half dead bird perched on your shoulder would be far creepier than a solitary, angry eye.

I slip my left arm behind me, hoping to keep her from seeing the bracelet that blocks her ability to call me to her. Luckily, she's far too intent on staring me down to notice. I'm not stupid, I know she's pissed at me, but I don't dare show any fear. At least not in front of my tweed-wearing-Nazi-historian. She's just going to have to wait till we're alone to rip into me. Wondering if she can talk to me though the bird makes me smile as I imagine her nails-on-a-chalkboard voice emanating from its beak. Too bad she doesn't find any humor in the current situation. Claws dig into my shoulder, a reminder of how displeased she is with me.

Skinny-boy's prominent Adam's apple bobs when I return my attention to him. "You… you have a way with birds, Miss Fey."

Yeah, I'm a regular Snow White.

The curious tilt to his head and slow smile tell me he isn't seeing what I'm seeing. To him the only thing out of the ordinary about my shoulder ornament is that it's sitting there.

I pull the much hated, cell phone from my pocket and glance at the time. A watch would be more convenient and far less annoying. My shoulder lowers slightly with the piercing pressure of Hel's little helper. I need to take care of this now, before she leaves more permanent marks on my body.

"I guess you could say that, or they're more domesticated from hanging out on the Trail. People leaving scraps behind, feeding them, whatever. Can we continue our conversation at another time?"

"Oh, of course." Faltering fingers pull another card from his blazer pocket—Seriously, how is he withstanding the heat? Sweat is practically raining down his face—and holds it out toward me. "Call me any time."

Slipping the phone into my back pocket before reaching for the card, I nod. All the jostling sends the tiny bird claws a little deeper, but better that than waving the bracelet around. The last thing I need is her recognizing it as something that keeps her from contacting me. "Will do."

"I mean it, any time, day or night. It's never too late or too early."

I wave a hand in the air in answer as I turn,

not bothering to give him a chance to keep talking. Something tells me he won't stop. Making my way through the throng of early-evening hikers and bikers, I softly whisper to my companion, "Don't you think hanging on my shoulder is a little suspicious? Or is this how you get your shits and giggles nowadays?"

The damn thing pecks at my head.

"What the—" I pull back sharply, turning to look at the bird. Hel's one good eye glaring, a few silvery hairs hanging from the bird's beak. Bitch is on the tip of my tongue, but I manage to keep it behind my lips.

Reaching the edge of the bridge, my right butt cheek starts vibrating and *Sun King* by The Cult blasts from my pocket. Damn phone. Pulling it out, I tap the power button and ignore the call. Cell phones, especially ones smarter than you, are a pain in the ass.

Once I've stepped onto solid ground, Hel-bird lets loose a guttural coo and flies off, circling back to perch on the rail of the bridge. Chest puffed, head bobbing like she wants me to back up. Maybe there's something to this Iowa's Stonehenge thing and the supposed gateway to other worlds. If she's stuck there, I'm staying on this side. I don't have the time, patience, or brain power to deal with her right now.

The tingle of vibrations crosses my palm and

Sun King blares to life again. Hel I can ignore, but this I can't, at least not again. Answering her harsh screeches with a flippant wave, I turn and tap the answer icon.

"What do you want, Var?"

"Have I caught you at a bad time?"

"Yes, make it short, what do you want?"

"Did you receive the flowers?"

"Yeah, they're on the kitchen table." Rotting, alongside your half-assed apology. "What do you want, Var?"

"The pleasure of your company this evening."

"I'm bus—"

"I will pick you up at seven, wear something formal."

The call clicks off.

Asshat. Didn't even give me a chance to turn him down. I'm so tired of others planning my day for me. Training, kowtowing to Var Royd, work... The list goes on and on. I need a vacation away from everyone. Fat chance that'll happen.

Eyeing the bird on its perch, I frown and walk to the line dividing the bridge and its mystical portal with the real world.

"I know you're listening, Hel, and if I'm wrong... well your little messenger can carry this back to you. I've done what you wanted, I took the job, so stop bugging me."

Hel-bird cocks its head then does a little

bobbing dance in response. That crystal blue eye still glaring at me.

"I've got a lot on my schedule. I'll contact you when I'm good and ready. Right now, I'm not good or ready."

Hikers and bikers give me wide berth, I don't need to be an empath to feel the fear and uncertainty radiating off of them. Uns probably assume I'm crazy or drunk. Ens assuming the same, but for different reasons. Talent related reasons, I can see the recognition in some of their eyes. Yes, I look like a crazy woman chatting with a bird, but right now I don't care. I will later, but not for looking crazy.

Chapter 12

Wilted and sad, the roses still lay on my table. I should have tossed them and the bullshit apology card when I went out earlier. *Forgive me.* Words, just words, with no meaning behind them. Hel, he probably doesn't even remember why he's asking for forgiveness. I've heard them all too frequently from Var Royd. *Face it, Keely, you're in a one-sided abusive relationship.* He's like a parasite that's latched on and can't be removed by conventional means.

What the hel does he have planned that I need to wear something formal? I'm half tempted to wear the grungiest clothes I can find. A nasty, raggedy old teeshirt and jeans reserved for cleaning the shop or house. I've already ticked of the goddess of the underworld, why not piss off the Sun King too? Gods, they're notoriously fickle and I haven't met one that doesn't think Carly's song is about them.

I pull the cell phone from my pocket and toss it next to the deteriorating roses. I've avoided the nasty contraptions since conception. Shutting out the world for chunks at a time is important to me and now nearly impossible.

I'm now the Lord's Shadow. A difficult concept to wrap my head around, even weeks after the deed. I don't think I'll ever get used to it and maybe that's a good thing. Getting used to it could lead me down a dangerous path. One I've walked before. One that's hard to deny once you're on it.

I'd been forced to choose a side in the swirling shit storm surrounding me and had three choices Var Royd, Hel, or Stasia Athory. I chose what seemed to be the easiest path.

Stasia hadn't been a big enough fish in the pond to even consider. I see that now. I also see my fear of her was unsubstantiated. It doesn't matter that she is half demon, or that her mother was the infamous Blood Countess. She had no way of releasing Einen, hel, she doesn't know where he's being held. Neither do I for that matter. As for forcing me to donate blood? She's going to have to rethink her anti-wrinkle cream formula. Of course this might be the hubris of my newly acquired position talking.

The job is like a get out of jail free card. Literally. There's no way the NTF—the Numinous Task Force, an agency set up to police Enchants—can touch me now, not as long as I stay the course and pretend to be Var's favorite pet. They'll have to pin Stanley Lewis's disappearance on someone else. After all, I didn't make him disappear, I delivered him to his victims. They got their vengeance and although I'm no longer in the CU—as I should be, considering I helped kill someone—I'm paying in other ways. Membership in this elite circle has its privileges and its pitfalls, one being this freakin' cellphone.

Had I been up on my Germanic history, I would have recognized Vanadís and Ingvarr as pseudonyms for who they truly are, the gods Frey and Freya. The Sisters, my grandmother and great aunts, had done their best to hide me from them. If the block they'd placed on my Talents hadn't worn off, I'd still be off their radar. This doesn't excuse my irritation with The Sisters and the cover ups, but they are my family, even if it's not by blood. As unpredictable as Var Royd and his sister are, they are still more predictable than Hel.

Bits and pieces of our past conversations float to the surface of my foggy brain. Hel encouraged me to accept the new position. Had I not really *chosen* a side at all? Had I stepped into something much larger? Something much more dangerous? After all, I still owe her a favor. One she's not going to let slide, not that I expect her to. If it weren't for her, I probably wouldn't be alive today. Stanley "The Collector" Lewis would now own my Talents and I'd be worm food. But that doesn't mean I'm going to jump every time she snaps her fingers.

If I wasn't a plaything of the gods before, I'd cemented my position as Shadow by word, if not intention. My bestie, Annya, warned me about intention and binding spells. The intention behind the words is the key. Unlike when I'd agreed to Hel's conditions for help, I'd been so focused on parroting Var Royd's words, the intent behind them hadn't even crossed my mind. No, that's a lie. I'd never wanted the job and my inner Keely had fought tooth and nail against the words and their meaning. The whole mess is a hard learned lesson in never say never.

Now I have a whole new problem. Mr. I'm-not-a-Nazi Mort offering help to help me. Part of me wants to run screaming in the other direction, but it's a much smaller piece than the one fueled by curiosity.

Warm fur winds its way around and through my ankles, a little less than the full pressure of twenty pounds pushing against me. Crouching down, I scratch CC behind the ears. "I've brought this all on myself, haven't I?"

What his golden-green eyes don't say, his yawn does.

"Thanks for helping cheer me up."

He yawns again and I find myself copying. After yesterday's training, today's meeting with Mort and run in with Hel, I'm exhausted. Too exhausted to deal with Var and his fancy-schmancy plans for the evening, but there's no getting out of that. One can only hope it includes dinner. A girl's gotta eat, might as well be on someone else's dime.

The big hand on the clock points to twelve and the little one to four, plenty of time for a nap.

"Come on, fur ball, let's go crash on the couch for a bit."

CC jumps up next to me as I flip through channels on the T.V., pausing as a familiar face graces the screen. "Hello." Sliding to the edge of the couch, I hold the volume button until Haydn Koehler's smoky, sweet voice fills the room.

"—continues to discriminate against Enchants."

"But, Mr. Koehler, isn't it true that Ens don't have a need for health coverage?" asks the perky little reporter. "Several of you *are* immortal, or close to it."

He places a hand on her shoulder, tilting his head to the side, and smiles. "Immortal does not mean we are invincible."

"Condescending ass." I tear my attention from the screen long enough to glance down at CC. "Am I right?"

His little head swivels toward the T.V. and back, then he yawns and butts his head against my arm.

"I know, I know, you wanna cuddle. Hold on just a sec." I turn my attention back to my *assignment* as he mentions my boss.

"The name of Var Royd's company explains where his interests lie and it's hardly with the healthcare of Uns." The smirk on Koehler's face is a strange cross between endearing and annoying.

"Anbetung has a special meaning?"

"Yes, it's German for worship."

"Thank you Mr.—"

I hit the off button and flop backward, an open invitation for a cat to crawl onto my lap. "Hel's Realm, is that name intentional, or a total screw up like his choice of last name? Seriously, who the hel *picks* a name like Royd?"

CC's motor runs full throttle as he watches me from under drooping lids.

"I know, you don't give a shit, but I have to at least give half of one considering he's my boss. He really needs to learn to do his research before naming things." I run a hand over the cat's head and back. "Although, I can see him choosing worship on purpose. Hemorrhoid is totally into having everyone bow down to him. Hel, these *worshipers* even pay him for the honor."

I glance at the clock. In less than three hours I get the fantabulous honor of spending the evening with Des Moines' biggest pain in the ass. So much for a quick nap, there's no way I'll be able to shut my brain off now.

Chapter 13

My hair is pulled back in a sleek ponytail, because it's all I can mange. The shower felt so good I didn't want to get out, and well, to be honest, I'm having a bad hair day. Yes, hairstylists have bad hair days too, more often than you'd think. Ponies can be formal, when done right.

As for formal dress, the only thing in my closet that comes close is my senior prom dress, and there's no way in hel I'm pulling that out. Instead, I keep it simple, a white, ankle length sheath, my Hel deterrent bracelet, and hoops. For an extra bit of drama, I thread the moonstone onto a chain, smirking as I remember Var's reaction when Ric gave it to me. If he truly is interested in me as more than one of his tools, this should bug him all night. Hel, maybe he'll cancel dinner and I'll get to chill at home, just me, the cat, and some brainless TV.

The buzzer sounds as I put the finishing touches on my face, a little powder and redder-than-red lips. What possessed me to pick red lipstick? It will probably end up all over my face and teeth, but it's too late to change it now. I take my time tossing touchup products in my evening bag and grab a silk wrap that matches my lips. Yeah, it's August, but it lends a bit of pizazz.

"I'm coming, I'm coming," I mutter, as the buzzer sounds again. Pushing the button, I refrain from screaming, "I'll be down in a minute."

"Yes, Miss Fey."

"Jeffery?" I immediately feel bad about making him wait, I like Var's chauffeur. His driving skills are amazing, I know from the night we spent eluding a mysterious car that turned out to be the NTF trailing me. Because, surprise, they think I'm behind Stanley Lewis's disappearance, little do they know how right they are. And Jeffery is a nice guy, unlike his boss.

"Yes, ma'am."

"You alone?"

"Yes, if it wouldn't be too much trouble could we continue this conversation in the car? Mr. Royd left orders to have you back by no later than a quarter till."

"I'm on my way." Had I known Jeffery was picking me up I wouldn't have been so petty, the last thing I want to do is get him in trouble. "Hold down the fort, CC."

Locking both conventional and magical locks on my apartment—one can never take too many precautions—I hustle as fast as my backless, two-inch kitten heels allow. Those who don't wear them, have no idea how hard it is to navigate on heels of any height, especially when they're held on by one thin strap across the toe. A fast pace, on stairs, is a disaster waiting to happen, one I manage to avoid.

Jeffery is standing at the door and pulls it open as soon as the lock is undone. His friendly smile turns to something more akin to awe as I step outside. "You look lovely, Miss Fey."

I remember why I wore the red lipstick, as my lips become the focal point. It's been my experience that men either hate lipstick or love it, with red being the number one choice among those that love it. Red screams passion, sensuality, and danger. To me it screams power and confidence. Anytime I need a little boost in the confidence arena, I slap on a little red. And tonight I need all the confidence I can get.

Feeling like a real femme fatale, I return his smile. "Thanks, Jeffery, should we get going? I don't want to get you in trouble."

"Yes, yes of course." He shakes his head, as if trying to clear it, and opens the limo's door for me.

Frowning, I look at the open door and expansive emptiness it reveals. "Mind if I sit up front with you?" My powerful, red lipstick moment has passed. No matter how many times I ride in Var's limo, I can't get over feeling funny sitting in the back by myself.

He hesitates, forehead crinkled, mouth opening

and closing, and then shakes his head. "I don't know, Miss Fey, if Mr. Royd would see—"

"He's not going to see, we'll stop a block or two away and I'll switch seats, if it's going to cause problems."

He hesitates, hand still on the door.

"And stop calling me Miss Fey, you and I are on the same level, we're both employees."

With a quick push the back door swings shut and he opens the passenger side door. "As you wish, Keely."

I pat his shoulder and quickly climb inside, so he can shut to door, I know better than to tell him I can handle it. We might be equal in my eyes, but Jeffery still takes his orders and his job seriously.

"His lordship still calling you James?" Var gets his kicks saying "Home, James" to Jeffery.

He chuckles as we take the exit onto highway 141. "It still amuses him and if he's amused, I have a job."

"Your job should be contingent on your performance—which is superb, if you ask me—not Var's amusement."

He shrugs. "As long as my paycheck has my real name on it, he can call me whatever he wants."

"Well, if you're okay with it."

"I am, this job is far better than driving a taxi."

I drop the subject, concentrating on the scenery, until we come to the stop lights in Granger. "Don't suppose you know what he has planned for me this evening. If we're going to dinner why didn't he come along?"

Jeffery stares at me and a car behind us honks, signaling the light change. His lips press into a thin line as he takes his foot off the brake and eases ahead. The car behind us pulls up alongside, and teenage heads hang out the window, shouting and flipping us the bird before squealing away.

"Damn, kids," I mutter. You know you're getting old when your view changes from damn old people to damn kids.

Jeffery keeps his eyes on the road, the whiteness of his knuckles and ridged jaw screams nervous, and I don't think it has anything to do with the carload of rude teens.

"Am I to take it you don't know?"

He shakes his head. "My orders were to have you at his place by a quarter to eight."

"Jeffery, you're an awesome driver, but a lousy liar."

"It's not my place, Miss Fey."

"Oh, stop it with the Miss Fey crap. If you can't tell me, you can't tell me."

"I'm sorry." He glances over at me as we take the ramp onto the interstate.

Sighing, I press myself back into the seat, crossing my arms over my chest. In truth, he never said we were going out to dinner—wish I'd eaten

more at lunch or shoved a candy bar in my bag—
maybe this some kind of elaborate set up to get
me alone. Great, a night of Var trying to seduce
me. Hopefully, I'm strong enough to ward off the
warm fuzzies he projects when he wants something.
He's used it on me before and all I wanted was to
bask in the feeling of being loved and would have
done anything he asked, if I hadn't come to my
senses. Having to do the walk of shame from my
boss's apartment is the last thing I need.

Chapter 14

Both of my guesses as to what tonight will hold are way off base. No dinner, at least not in the conventional sense. There is a table of finger foods, a small bar, and waiters readying large trays of drinks and hors d'oeuvres. I can't rule out seduction as of yet, but a cocktail party isn't exactly the time or place, unless he intends it to be an orgy. Perish the thought.

I've now got three guesses as to why I'm here. Arm candy—like there aren't hundreds of others who could fill that spot—as a show of Var's power, or he wants me to do something. More than likely, it's the latter. What that thing is, I'm about to find out.

The crowd of workers parts as Var makes his way toward me, a huge smile that doesn't quite jive with the calculating look in his eyes. "Keely, you look enchanting." He takes my hand, brushing his lips across it, before placing it on his arm and escorting me through the room.

Maybe I'm wrong and I am just arm candy for the night. "It would have been nice if you'd explained your little shindig."

"Would you have voluntarily agreed to attend?"

Umm, I didn't voluntarily agree to anything, you told me when to be ready. I keep my lips sealed and shrug.

He laughs and pats my hand. "Just as I thought."

"So why am I here? I highly doubt it's because you needed a date for your own party."

He laughs again and a chill runs down my spine. "Have I told you lately how much I enjoy your company?" he whispers, lips brushing against my ear, sending the chill back up my spine.

I freeze, like a deer mesmerized by headlights. Arm candy, check. Seduction, check. Why not go for the whole trifecta? Unclenching my jaw, I turn my head slightly. "Seriously, Var, why do you want me here? I'm sure there are thousands of women who'd willingly be your plus one, and your sister would make a much better hostess."

"You would not be the slightest bit jealous if I made another my 'plus one'?"

It's all I can do to keep from rolling my eyes. Talk about ego. "The thought hasn't crossed my mind."

"I am wounded," he says, brushing his lips against my ear again, "but you are correct, Vana is better suited to the part of hostess."

I inwardly fume, but steel my outward expression. Can't be mad when I'd stepped right into that one. I know perfectly well I'm not equipped to play hostess of a highbrow cocktail party, but that doesn't mean it doesn't sting.

"And you are quite right that I have a task for you, my dear." He steps back, gaze running the length of me.

Good grief, why is he always twisting things into a sexual nature? Or is it me? His eyes linger on my chest. Nope, it's him. The dark sensuality switches to irritation when it lands on the moonstone. Woohoo, point to Keely, a petty little point, but I'll take 'em where I can get 'em.

"Your task for the evening is to listen in on my guest's conversations." His tone and manner drop the ambience to sub-zero as he continues to stare at the charm.

"So you want me to wander around and eavesdrop on your guests?"

His eyes finally meet mine and I can't suppress the shiver. His eyes are stormy and winter cold instead of the usual sand and surf brilliance. I was hoping for miffed when I added the necklace, not pissed off. I really should stop poking the bear.

"No, I want you to use your Talents to listen in, that way they will not be the wiser." He begins to walk away and I should let him, but stupidity reigns supreme.

I grab his coat sleeve, tugging him back toward me. "How the hel do I do that?"

"You have been practicing your shadow craft

with my Sword and Shield, am I correct?" asks Var.

I nod. "But I haven't put the practice into practical use. What if I screw up?"

He turns, placing his hands gently on my shoulders. The start of a reassuring smile is squashed as his gaze lands on the moonstone again. I hadn't even noticed I was nervously twiddling with the damn thing. I drop my hand, but it's too late, I've kicked his ego. *Way to go, Keely.*

"For Vereinen it was a very simple task. One that even you, with your limited knowledge, should be able to accomplish."

The words are meant to hurt, but all they do is piss me off. I know I have *limited knowledge*, tell me something I don't know.

"Then maybe you should have asked Vereinen instead of me to handle this." The words are out of my mouth before common sense can kick in and stop them.

Darkness descends between us that has nothing to do with my Talents and everything to do with his pride. The gentle pressure of his fingers builds, biting into my shoulders until I gasp and attempt to pull back. He releases me, hands hovering over my shoulders. He opens his mouth then closes it before turning and stalking away.

Damn it, why do I insist on saying and doing things that only deepen the hole I'm in?

Chapter 15

Use your Talents to spy on my guests, he says. A simple task, he says. Yeah, right. If finding my center with Teiran huffing and puffing down my neck is difficult, finding it in a crowd of Ens is damn near impossible. There's too much going on. Too many faces to identify. Too much noise. Too much bodily contact. And way, way too much fear on my part.

What if I get caught? What if I trigger nasty shadow people to attack? What if I lose control and my influence over the dead affects Var's vamp guests? There are a million reasons not to use my Talents, but not a single one will get me out of having to *do my job.*

Meandering my way through the maze of guests and tray-bearing waitstaff, I glance longingly at the glasses filled with bubbling fun. What I wouldn't give to have a little liquid courage, but I need a different kind of bubbly. One that won't addle my brain. After all, I'm not here for fun, I've got a job to do.

The pretty bartender—Why is everyone Var hires pretty? You'd think he'd want a few who didn't compete in the looks department—flashes me a brilliant smile, but everything else about him is vacant. Maybe that's the ticket, pleasing on the outside, empty on the inside. "What can I get you?"

"Dr. Pepper, please."

Tall, handsome, and void makes a show of tossing some ice in a glass. "Sure you don't want anything in that? It's an open bar." He wiggles his brow and winks.

"I'm positive." He's pretty free with Var's money—not that my employer can't afford it, I just don't like how Pretty Vacant went about it— wonder if he would have grabbed the expensive stuff, or stuck to the cheap house brand.

He shrugs, opens a can, and pours the contents into the glass. Stashing the can under the counter, he sets the glass in front of me. "One virgin Dr. Pepper," he says, holding out his hand.

I fight to keep the frown from my face, and the "thought this was an open bar" tightly behind my lips. When I don't respond, he motions toward a tip jar. Working in the service industry I'm a harsh judge when it comes to tipping. Do your job, be pleasant, don't dis your employer with customers, and most of all don't act as if you're owed a tip. I know the importance of tips and had he not been so blatant, I might have added to the green in his jar.

Grabbing my glass, I turn and before I can take my first step I hear, "Stingy bitch." Now I'm doubly glad I didn't tip him, and hope no one else does. Actually, there might be a way I can make that happen. I'll kill two birds with one stone, work on practicing my Talent in a room full of people and have a little fun with the ill-mannered bartender. Receiving a few strange looks and some raised brows as I make my way through the crowd, I wipe the smile from my face. Need to work on my poker face.

Stepping into a quiet corner with a view of the bar, I take a deep breath and work on finding my center. The hardest part is keeping my eyes open, the last thing I need is to telegraph I'm doing something. Especially if that something will freak out Var's guests and negate my mission. All the noise and movement—not to mention the fear of someone discovering what I'm doing—constantly pulls at my attention. Maybe I should have gotten a shot of something in my soda.

I shift gears to people-watching and notice a few familiar faces, including the Mayor, a couple of councilmen, and some movers and shakers from the business world. No one I've met or know personally, but I've seen them in the paper or on TV from the upper echelons of Des Moines society. And some of them are starting to notice me. For all I know, they think I'm part of the party package. Come for the drinks and hors-d'oeuvres, leave with a bedtime snack.

Suppressing a shudder, I take a drink and plaster a smile on my face. One that hopefully says, *I'm waiting for someone and it's not you.* From the looks I'm getting it's coming off more like, *there's something not right about that girl.* Either way, it's working, no one approaches me.

Taking a calming breath, I reach down into myself and search for the mythical place Ric calls my center. That certain body part that houses an En's Talent. These parts are what The Collector took from his victims—a healer's hands, a fortuneteller's eyes, and a variety of others—literally disenchanting them.

Ric's been teaching me to use this 'center' as my focus. Having a focus is supposed to help me have control over my Talents, but I can't seem to locate my center. Maybe I don't have one central place where my Talents live. To hel with finding my center, if it hasn't worked in the past, it's not going to work now. It's time to try something different.

Every time I purposely use my Talents—hair growth, nail lengthening, or skin exfoliation—I don't focus on my Talents, I concentrate on what I'm doing. If my task is to grow someone's hair, I concentrate on the hair. Why would it be any different with shadows?

I concentrate on the small shadow cast by the tip jar. Staring intently is as bad as closing my eyes, but it can't be helped. Besides, I'm not staring at *anyone*, just the bar. If I look like a drunk, who cares? I push my worries and doubts to the side and will the shadow to answer me. A little wiggle or twitch would be nice, some kind of indication it *hears* me, but nada.

Exhaling, I glance around the room to see if anyone has noticed my little experiment. There's only one set of eyes targeted on my corner. Vibrant sapphire blue eyes watch me without even a hint of acknowledgement, but he knows I see him. A small shiver races along my skin, a combo of fear and lust. Breaking contact, I search the room for his golden counterpart. Where there's a Shield, there's usually a Sword.

Chapter 16

I spot Ric directly across the room from Teiran and the shiver, minus the fear, intensifies. Lord Ingvar's Shield and Sword have been working together since… hel, I don't know, the dawn of time? In the past, they worked as a trio with my Shadow counterpart, Vereinen, at least until he supposedly went crazy and tried to overthrow Var. I don't totally believe Einen—who I'd labeled an imaginary childhood friend before my life took a tumble and I found out he's real—could be as bad as everyone makes him out to be. Sure, he can be a dick, but it's possible—like yours truly—he couldn't control his Talents. Although I can see where having Talents like ours could drive you insane. I've been on that precipice before and managed to keep myself from plummeting into the abyss.

The three of us are supposed to be working as a team, but I can't help wonder if they are here to watch me, or merely in their usual capacity as protection for Var. Doesn't matter, I have a job to do. Putting my gorgeous, âlfar—Teiran hates it when I use the Americanized elf to describe us—bookends on ignore, I get back to it.

With all the people milling around the bar, it's nearly impossible to get a clear, consistent view of the tip jar. I need a new focus target. Var's apartment is decorated in *tastefully sparse*—unlike my own eclectic hodgepodge—with only a handful of things that throw shadow besides the furniture. The last thing I want to do is use a chair someone is sitting in as my focus. I nearly giggle, imagining a shadow creeping out from under a piece of furniture and grabbing a guest's leg. That would add some excitement to this party.

I finally settle on an iridescent sculpture on a pedestal near me. Because of its twisted shape, there are plenty of shadowy bits to play with, and it'll be easier to hide what I'm doing under the guise of art appreciation. It's probably worth more than I make in a year, maybe two. Let's hope playing with its shadow doesn't knock it over.

Studying the shape and contours of the piece, I chose the largest shadow at the base. Bigger might be easier. Taking a deep breath, I squelch the desire to use my fingers to beckon the darkness. I'm supposed to be admiring a piece of art, not coaxing a dog. I cross my arms over my chest, one hand still clutching the nearly full glass of soda, the other supporting my elbow. Pushing away the distractions of the party, I focus on the shadow and call to my Talent as if this were a simple hair lengthening service.

My lids droop and lips compress into a tight line—gods, I hope I don't end up with red lipstick all over my face—as the slow building tingle rides along my flesh. My skin starts to feel tight, constricting, like a trash compactor squishing my innards.

"Move, damn it," I whisper, exhaling and sucking in another breath. The tingle turns to an itch that can't be scratched, intensified by a thin layer of sweat. Great, smeared makeup and BO. All I need now is a case of bedhead and wrinkled clothes. That would give everyone something to talk about.

I push my will onto the stubborn shade under the sculpture. Is that…? Did it…? There's the smallest of movements. I beckon it again, hoping I didn't hallucinate, that it wasn't a change in the lighting. This time there's no mistake, it moves down the pedestal, nearly reaching the floor.

An arm wraps around my shoulders and I jump, splashing Dr. Pepper over everything within proximity. "Damn it, Var," I say, turning to the owner of the arm. "That's twice you've made me spill something by sneaking up on me." The first time had been at my client and friend, Lorelei's Solstice party, he'd made me dump a plate of stuffed mushrooms and a glass of bubbly.

His laughter fans my anger, but the leering gaze as he takes in my disheveled appearance swiftly turns it to embarrassment. "If memory serves me, you were wearing white that night too."

I don't bother telling him it wasn't white I was wearing. What's the point?

He clicks his fingers and one of the waiters appears with a towel. Surprisingly, he gently wipes at the sticky, brown liquid covering me. I would have thought I'd have been last on the list of things to be cleaned, his possessions would have been first. Then again, in his mind, I am one of his possessions. The towel is tossed to the waiter, who without question proceeds to wipe up the mess dotting the sculpture, pedestal, and floor.

Steering me away from the mess he smiles. "I apologize, I only came over to congratulate you on your progress."

"You've been watching me?" Duh, of course he's been watching me.

"You are mastering your Talents quite well."

"But I haven't been able to use them to do what you asked."

He waves a hand, brushing away my words. "You have done well controlling your Talent in a room full of people, without drawing undue attention. What more could I ask at this stage?"

Oookay, am I talking to a doppelgänger? Because this sure doesn't sound like the Var Royd I talked to earlier. Visions of The Collector disguised as my co-worker, Rey, flood my brain. He'd used

Rey's form to trick me into going with him, so he could kidnap me and steal my Talents. I glance around the room looking for the real Var Royd. I do not want to be duct-taped and thrown into a trunk again, ever.

Continuing to direct me away from the crowd, he frowns. "You look as if I am going to beat you."

"Well, I kinda figured you'd be pissed off that I didn't collect any juicy gossip." Secretly, I'm glad he doesn't expect more. Manipulating shadows is harder than manipulating hair, and I'm tired. Exhausted to be exact, all I want to do is crawl into bed. After I wash off my sticky soda shower. Speaking of which, I really need to find the bathroom and attempt to clean up.

He laughs, that deep, sensual kind that sets a body quivering. "The lack of *juicy gossip* aside, you did very well tonight. All that I ask is that you continue practicing on the subject of your assignment."

"Haydn Koehler."

"Yes, Haydn Koehler, I want regular updates on your progress."

So much for me thinking he's concerned about my wellbeing.

Lifting a hand, he motions and Ric appears. "Escort Miss Fey to the garage. She's had a long night."

"Yes, my lord," says Ric. A smile plays at the

corners of his lips and Var's hold on me tightens.

Var's eyes narrow as Ric holds out his hand to me. "When you have delivered her, hurry back, I need you here."

Smile wiped from his face, Ric nods. "Yes, my lord."

Before Var releases his hold, he leans down, and I turn my head so his lips brush against my cheek. "Goodnight, *my* Schattenkind."

I ignore the emphasis on my and nod. "Goodnight, Var." I refuse to call him 'my lord' and luckily he hasn't demanded it. The day that happens things will be a lot less peachy between us, as if they're wonderful now.

Chapter 17

"Thank you for *escorting* me to meet Jeffery." I shake my head at Ric's puzzled look. "Jeffery, Var's chauffeur."

"James," I mumble when he still doesn't get it. "I've told you this before. His real name is Jeffery, but Var gets off on saying 'home, James' so he calls him James."

"Ahh. It's not as if walking with you to the garage is a burden." He gives me a brilliant, turn-the-knees-to-jello smile.

"Whoa, wait a minute, did I hear you use a contraction?"

"Did I? I blame your influence." He winks and steps onto the elevator.

Smiling, I follow and lightly punch his arm. "Keep taking baby steps and you might make it into the current century. Of course by then you'll have learn a whole new one."

His laughter is warm and sweet, like a summer's day. Almost everything about him reminds me of summer, but that's part of being a liosâlfar, or light elf. They all have tanned complexions and light eyes and hair. Something to do with their kingdom residing in the sky. I don't know if that's true, having never bothered to ask. The tiny difference with Alric is his complexion isn't a true tan, more of a light honey, and he has fangs. I don't know the whole story of how he became a vamp, something to do with Nazis and Var's ex-wife, Trudy. I do know his elven heritage is what allows him to walk around during the day.

"Ladies first," he says, as the elevator doors open.

We make our way through the skywalk in blissful silence, giving me plenty of time to ponder why Var sent me home early. His orders had been to spy on his guests, yet he sends me home after observing me playing with the shadows. Was this just a test to see if I could manipulate them? I guess I did hold it together rather well in a room full of strangers. No stray shadow monsters materializing to eat his guests, no calling the dead or controlling vampires. Not a single slip-up. Yay, team Keely.

Ric holds the door for me, I step over the threshold and stop. The parking garage is quiet, not a living soul in sight, just vehicles. I assume most belong to Var's guests. Yet, the hair on the back of my neck stands at attention. I know there are security cameras, but the fist of intuition grasps my stomach. Something, or someone is keeping an eye on us that has nothing to do with building security.

"Ric," I whisper, reaching for his arm. "There's someone out there, and I don't think it's security." Why can't I have one day without some form of danger lurking around the corner?

There's an almost undetectable sound of two objects rubbed together and from the corner of my eye I see the faint glow of Ric's sword. If we make it through whatever awaits us in the shadows of the garage, I've got to ask him where he hides that thing. Wait, shadows, that's my territory. I was able to manipulate them tonight, maybe I can rearrange them a bit so we can see what's out there.

Ric grabs my arm with his free hand and begins pulling me into the open space. I dig my heels in, pulling backward. Turning, he frowns and jerks his head to the side. I give him the universal stop motion with my hand, then point toward the wall by the doors. See, I pay attention, always keep your back to the wall when possible. Slowly, we back up and over, when we reach the wall I lean against it for support.

What the hel are you doing? Ric's question pushes into my mind.

Working. Now shut up and let me concentrate. I slam a brick into my mental wall shutting out his concern and frustration. This is one of those times I'm grateful for his ability to communicate this way. It probably won't be the last, but right now I need to focus on finding what's out there.

Picking one shadow isn't going to be enough, there are too many for who or whatever is out there to hide behind. One corner of my mind is whining about being tired and scared, another answers with shut up and put on your big girl panties. This could be a life or death situation. I need to channel that fear—something we discovered early on was a Talent trigger—to use my Talent. Not the tiny bit I let trickle out at Var's party, I need a lot more, a whole lot more.

Taking a deep breath, I close my eyes as I let it out. That familiar slow tingle builds from my feet upward until my body is buzzing with power. Control is a hazy thing as I lift the hatch containing my Talent and everything comes rushing back. I haven't been this open to its power since my run in with The Collector. I feel Ric's hand on my arm and for a brief moment I second-guess my decision, but it's too late now.

I shake off his hand as the power wraps itself around me like an old friend, enlightening me to everything I am, everything I could be, and everything I've been when I set it free. That sensation of utter control over all things in my life is tantalizing. No more Var. No more Hel. I'd be free. Free to do and be whatever I want. So tantalizing I want to give in, let the power guide me to this promise of freedom.

Something warm grasps my arm, my attention

swings from the shadows and all they promise to Ric. How dare he interfere? Anger joins desire.

"Calm yourself, Keely."

I glare at him, all that I desire is within my grasp, why should I listen to Var's toy?

"Do no let the power control you."

The temptation to show him who's in control grips me and I raise my hand. He has two choices, let go of my arm and back away, or use his sword and kill me. Either way, we find out who's in control.

"Killing the liosâlfar will solve nothing, little Schattenkind."

Ric lets go of my arm, raising his sword. I feel my way through shadow and shade, locating the owner of the familiar voice.

"You," I whisper, the heady feeling of power washed down the drain by fear.

"Yes, me." The discordance of Hel's voice matches her appearance. Beauty and decay. Seductive sweetness and nails on a chalkboard.

"What are you—"

"Doing here? You have been ignoring me, little Schattenkind."

"I've been busy."

Ric sidles closer, covering the arm that wears the bracelet.

"I do not appreciate your callous disregard of my messengers." There's a strain to her stance and her tone is that of an elder chastising a child, anger barely held in check.

Déjà vu anyone? First Var and now Hel, I seem to be destined to repeat myself when it comes to certain situations.

"I also do not appreciate whatever steps you have taken to keep me from summoning you directly." Her form wavers, like bad TV reception. I open my mouth, then close it, no use trying to deny it. I only hope she doesn't figure out what's blocking her signal.

Ric steps forward, attempting to shield me from Hel. Not that it will do any good if she wants me. "What is it you want?"

My ears flinch as she laughs. I have the urge to touch her so only the pleasing notes can escape her mouth. My touch erases the decay, leaving only exquisite beauty. It's a wonder she didn't want to keep me in Helheim as her personal stylist. She probably would have, if I didn't have the power to enthrall her subjects.

"Frey's puppet speaks," she says, shaking her head. "I want nothing, Liosâlfar, but to give the little schattenkind a message."

Her words are becoming as blurred and fuzzy as her physique. Common sense indicates she's having problems maintaining the tether between this and the otherworld, giving me a huge advantage. If it's true. I grow a little bolder, stepping to the side, but still keep Ric between us. I may be dumb, but I'm not stupid.

"Consider it received."

She smiles—the side of her face that has lips smiles, the other side is all bared teeth and rotting flesh, making it beyond disturbing— and steps back, disappearing into the shadows.

Chapter 18

With possible Nazis on the right of me and gods on the left, it's no wonder sleep evades me. I've had a very full day. You'd think I'd be exhausted and I am, but sleep is a fleeting, wishful dream, one I wish I could achieve. Instead, I'm left tossing and turning, disturbing the easy sleep of a cat. Why can he sleep through almost anything? Is it because he's learned to let things go, whereas I cling to every little issue?

Stroking his grey and white fur helps me relax and he doesn't seem to mind. In fact, he's stretched himself across my midsection, holding me in place. I don't dare move, no matter how much body parts ache to change position, for fear of nasty glares from golden green eyes and a severe chastising in cateese.

I need to take a lesson from CC and let the previous day's troubles go. But when you add up the complications of my life, it's almost too much to handle. The boy in tweed claims to have access to old Nazi research explaining what I am. My new boss, who happens to be the god Frey, has ordered me to figure out how to use my Talents to spy on a professional protestor with a grudge against him. I'm always on the look out for the NTF, wondering if they're going to put two and two together and figure out I killed Stanley Lewis. There's also the guilt over that, I'll never forget the look on his face when the dead rose to take him. And let's not forget the two-faced goddess Hel, who has a different kind of hold on me, in the form of a favor owed.

Somehow, most of these things are tied together, I just haven't figured out how and why. Without sleep I won't be figuring anything out. If I could get to sleep I might stand a chance of contacting Einen. When I had the collar on, I didn't dare, not without the fear of being decapitated. Now the only thing holding me back is not knowing where to find him. I've searched and there's no sign of him, not even a whisper on the wind. Var and his twin Vana—the goddess Freya—have hidden him somewhere.

I need to figure out where.

He's the one person who knows how to control the shadows and those idiots have denied me access to him. I don't see either of them jumping up to help me learn, instead, Var dumps my training in Ric and Teiran's laps. They know what I'm capable of, but neither know the fine details of how to put my Talents into practice. Not to mention the massive resentment between them and schattenkind Talents. I can't blame Ric after tonight.

The glowing numbers on the clock flip to eight a.m., five hours left before I have to get up. I can manage on five hours, but the clock keeps ticking down. Pretty soon we'll hit the point where I can't manage.

I'm not one of those Ens who can survive on limited or no sleep. Without sleep simple things become difficult and the difficult become impossible. Things start to fail, especially control. Control over temper. Control over what comes out of my mouth. Control over my Talents. The most recent being my little encounter in the parking garage, I'd contemplated killing Ric. He's done nothing to deserve it. Except maybe the whole finding me in The Between after I'd offed The Collector—I try and think of him as Stanley, but it's easier not too. Now I know why killers refuse to give their victims names, it's easier to think of them as a thing, instead of a person—and dropping me off at the CU, The Enchant Containment Unit, was not a pleasant place to wake up.

The only thing worse than not being able to sleep is being alone with your thoughts. In my case, the two may go hand in hand. Unhinged, exhausted laughter bubbles up and out, and paws prod and push me into a more comfortable cat cushion, reminding me I'm not alone.

"Sorry, fur ball, I'm not a very good cuddle buddy right now." He yawns and I scratch behind his ears. His little pink nose scrunches as I scratch along his jaw and under his chin.

"Too bad you can't help me with the mess I've gotten myself into."

He crosses his paws over my belly. In the alarm clock's soft glow, I see him tilt his head to one side and open his mouth in a silent meow.

"Yeah, I know, you told me so."

Gold and green eyes narrow.

"I don't need to speak cateese to understand that look. Pity I can't though, I'd really like your take on everything."

His little ears turn as if he hears something on the other side of the room. Faster than I can process it, CC is at the foot of the bed, hissing and growling at the corner of the room.

"Hel's realm, what's up with you?" I sit up and fear grasps me in its giant hand, forcing the oxygen from my lungs. In the deepest recesses of the far corner of the room, shadows waver and slither across the walls and ceiling. "What the fuck?"

Scrambling across the bed, I grab CC around his arched middle and roll out onto the floor, taking the sheets with me. Clutching the hissing, struggling cat to my chest, I scramble for the door, kicking the tangled sheets loose as I roll over the threshold. Struggling to my knees, I reach up and slam the door. Whatever that is, it's staying in there. I hope.

Curtains. Open the curtains. Light, lots of light will banish shadow. That or total darkness, but I don't have Teiran's Talent of creating absolute dark. Right about now, I wouldn't mind still having him as a roomy. Still clinging to my cat, I open all the drapes, until the living room and kitchen are flooded by dawn's early light.

Panic tells me to leave the apartment and head downstairs to Dara's. Sensibility questions if it's a manifestation of my own Talents. I may be tired, but I didn't create or *call* that thing, not that I haven't unwittingly done so in the past, but my control has gotten better. I've learned to heed the signs, anger, fear, the slow building itch and tightness of my skin. There was none of that this time, only me wallowing in my sorrows and the feeling of helplessness as I flounder for answers. Answers that feel just out of reach. Like the word you want on the tip of your tongue, but can't seem to spit out.

CC's reaction was definitely not friendly. Not that he's ever been friendly to any of my Talent related mistakes. This is different, his response was, *the enemy is upon us.* Not, *get your shit together.* Very reminiscent of his waking me from dreams that felt too real, or when The Collector invaded my personal space. He was protecting his space and the person who makes sure he's fed.

My fur ball may be a warrior, but I'm a big ol' chicken. That bedroom door is staying closed until I have to get ready for work and I might take a flashlight with me. What better weapon against the dark than a battery powered light?

Chapter 19

I wake up in a puddle of drool, clutching the flashlight like a security blanket. Twenty pounds of grey and white fur sits on the edge of the couch staring at me. Panicked that I'd over slept, I push myself up triggering pounding in my head and a stiff neck, brought on by cramped position I'd fallen asleep in. I sigh in relief, seeing what my great-aunt Eliza calls her 'stories' on the TV. It must be mid to late afternoon.

The clock confirms I have a couple of hours to spare before I have to get ready for work. Might as well do something constructive, like feed the cat before he eats me. Coffee brewing and kibble in CC's bowl, a shower is next on my agenda. That entails entering the dreaded bedroom. My hand hovers over the doorknob, what am I forgetting? A flashlight, too bad it's in the bedside table.

"Oh, for crying out loud, open the damn door. The boogie man isn't going to attack in broad daylight." Saying it out loud doesn't make it true, because I know it isn't. Opening the door, I slip my hand inside and flip on the lights. I swallow my fear and take a tentative step inside.

The sheets mark a trail to the door, pillows everywhere, and I sure don't remember knocking the lamp over in my escape. I guess now is as good a time as any to replace the bedding. Taking it off is half the battle and most of that's already been done. Scooping it up, I toss it in a basket for later. Grabbing a tee and shorts, I head to the bathroom. I may not be able to scrub the ick of last night from my insides, but soap and hot water on the outside is a step in the right direction.

Clean of body and clearer of mind, I grab my first cup of the day. Nothing like a strong cup of coffee to help clear the cobwebs of the brain. With what I'm about to try, I need to be as clear as possible.

Usually in practice, Ric has me sit on the floor, but in the vein of last night's *try something different*, I clear a spot on the couch. Might as well be comfortable for my foray into the world of shadow craft. Chuckling at my own wit, or lack of, I set my mug on the coffee table and plop down on the couch.

Closing my eyes, I take a deep breath to clear my mind, but doubt moves in. Should I be doing this alone? What if I need Ric and Teiran to help me stop whatever I conjure? Last night's shadowy garage incident and the bedroom takeover prove I can't always rely on myself to keep it under control. Not that there's any proof I caused the bedroom problem.

"Damn it, if you're going to excel at anything you have to practice and sometimes that means going it alone."

If I fail, they can come pick up the pieces later, if there are any to pick up. But that's not going to happen, right? I need to be able to do this without any help. Failure is not an option if I want to find Einen. And I want—no, I *need* to find Einen and I certainly can't do that with Ric and Teiran hovering over me.

Taking a deep breath, I slowly let it out, close my eyes and start at my toes. I relax all ten digits and every muscle until they feel heavy and loose. Slowly ascending my body, I release the tension and tightness, from ankles to hips. By the time I reach my waist, the world and all its worries are shut out, and I drift into utter blankness. No fears, no anxiety, no thoughts of any kind, just blissful emptiness.

I know where I want to be, so I concentrate on what I remember of Einen's place. Fresh outdoorsy scents filter in, the greenness of grass, musty dirt, light freshness of dew… and roses. I smell roses. The warm, soft cushions under my rear are gone. Eyes still closed, my fingers run along smooth, cool stone. Crickets, birds and other outdoorsy critters fill the air with the music of nature. My wiggling toes no longer touch hardwood flooring, instead they pull strands from a thick carpet of what can only be grass.

Is it possible? I've been here in the past. I've tried to get back in the present, but something has always block the way. I look around and see no one to stop me from getting to the house beyond the gardens. I need to get to that house. I need to know if I'm really here. Really in Einen's gardens. Really at Einen's house.

Scrambling to my feet, I let them carry me as fast as bare feet can move over the land, through the bushes, across the stones and paving blocks. The house comes into view, closer and closer with each step. A third of the way there I need to stop and catch my breath.

Wish I was in better shape. Something to add to my to do list.

Being an Enchant doesn't mean we don't need to workout. We may live a very long time, but it doesn't excuse us from taking care of our bodies. Or out minds. Living as long as many of us do can lead to madness, or boredom, or both. I may be a baby in En years, but I've felt the pull of madness and can't imagine what it will feel like in a couple hundred years, as I watch everything around me change and wither away.

Thoughts like these won't do you any good. Get a move on, you don't know how long you have here.

Walking turns to a trot, picking up speed as the house grows closer. My feet are bruised and probably bleeding from running over the stones. My shorts and tee are damp with sweat. My heart is about to burst from my chest and my lungs burn with every breath. But I don't care, I've reached the doors. Wouldn't it be a kicker if they don't open? But they do and I burst into the main entrance.

"Einen?"

Quiet. It's so quiet. Too quiet. The only sound is the blood pounding in my ears. Cautiously, I make my way across the cool marble. I refuse to be the idiot who wanders into the abandoned house thinking everything will be just hunky dory. Maybe I should find a weapon, just in case. Who knows what Var and Vana might have planted here to keep him in and me out. There's a poker by the enormous fireplace in what I'd call the living room. Cliche, I know, but in a pinch it will work. Hope for the best, but be prepared for the worst.

Keep exploring the main floor or take the stairs? I opt for the stairs.

"Einen? Are you up here?" Clinging to the wall, I take the steps one at a time. No need to rush to my doom. "Come on, give me a sign."

I search the corners and off-shooting hallways for any movement, corporeal or otherwise. It's possible he could use our mutual Talent to send me a message. A motioning shadow, perhaps. Nothing. All the shadows stay static and there's no other sign of life. Even the exotic flowers decorating the hall are dried and crumbling. The house itself feels stale and unused, like it's been closed for a long time. Far longer than the last time I was here.

If I were Var and Vana what would I do with him?

I need to find his bedroom, but I can't remember which of the of rooms is his. Yeah, I've been there, a couple of times, but we didn't exactly enter in a conventional way. Poker ready, I fling the first door open. Nothing. I continue down the hall, poker up, fling the door open. Shampoo, rinse, repeat.

At the end of the first hall I stop, drop my makeshift weapon to my side and sag against the wall. There are two more wings. If I continue like this, it's going to take all damn day. I need a faster way.

I'm taking a chance here, but what's the use of having this Talent if I can't make it work for me? And what better place to practice? I can't hurt anyone but myself, and maybe Einen, but I'd bet my life he knows how to protect himself.

Sliding down the wall, I make myself comfortable on the floor. Closing my eyes, brick by metaphorical brick, I let my defenses down. Let the power rise and crawl across my skin. Skin constricts against muscle and bone. Painfully tight. I clamp down on the power to keep it from overtaking me. The pain passes, the itch recedes, replaced by a pleasurable caress. I don't have to see to know the shadows are alive.

Gently, I push my will toward them. Show them my desire. *The doors, open them. Find Einen.* I try not to flinch as my hair moves, tickling bare skin in the breeze caused by their movement. Fear is ever-present when dealing with my Talents, but nothing could have prepared me for what I see behind my eyelids.

Chapter 20

The hall. Another hall. All the halls. Doors. Rooms. Floors. Walls. It goes on and on, in a dizzying array of spinning, rushing movement. I'm doubled over on the floor, clinging to my head. Don't know how much more I can take. I try to focus, but it's impossible. Sight. Sound. Smell. Touch. Too many perspectives. Sensory overload.

Find Vereinen. Find Vereinen. Find Vereinen, echoes over and over. There's no shutting it out when it comes from inside my head.

I try and take back the power, but it won't come willingly. It's free and happily roaming every level of the house unfettered. I fight to put the bricks back as more continue to fall. If I don't regain control, my protective wall will be nothing but a pile surrounding me.

Huddled behind what's left of my metaphysical wall, I beg them to stop. They laugh. I beg them to come to me and they argue with logic. They do my bidding. I commanded them to find Einen. Can't argue with that, I did ask, but my brain is not made to process multiple entities at once. Again, they laugh. The sound screeches like nails on a chalkboard.

The power is yours. Take it. Use it. Bend it to your will.

Is that Einen? Hel? My inner schattenkind?

"Yes, mine. I'm supposed to control it, not the other way around, but I'm untrained."

Stop denying it, foolish girl, take the power.

"I don't deny I have it. I don't know how to use it."

The only way to learn is to practice.

Hel's realm, I flashback to when I was stuck in The Between. I'm arguing with myself. Once again I'm reminded of how schattenkind Talents supposedly drove Einen mad. Fear of falling into madness forever on the edges of my subconscious, far outweighing the fear of failure.

Pain increases with each view of the house and all it contents. If I don't rein the power in soon my brain will be a Jackson Pollock mural on the walls, ceiling, and floor of Einen's lovely mansion.

A heavy sigh pushes through the whispers of joy and laughter of my shadow minions. Part of me wants to give in, let them have their fun. What's left of my sanity—what I guess to be the other voice in my head—keeps me from letting go. It's my power. They are my minions. I'm supposed to be the one in control. Anger is buried beneath a layer of pain and fear.

Yes. Take your anger. Use it. Let it work to your advantage.

"I can't. It hurts." The frickin' little voice in my head is making it worse.

What you feel now is but a taste of what you will feel, if you do not regain control. Continue to hide behind your cowardice and you will know true pain. Pain that will make you beg for death.

"You're not helping the situation."

Perhaps they should have killed you when they had the chance. You are weak and foolish, not worthy of such power.

"If you recall, I never wanted it." The violence behind my words, rips at my throat and throbs in my ears.

Want or not, the Talent is yours. The only say you have in the matter is if you will rise above and master it, or fall into self-pity and despair, letting it master you. From the look of you, it will be the second. You have, after all, failed with your own life by allowing others to become your master.

"Fuck you! I've done the best I can with the hand I've been given."

It was not given to you, you chose the paths you took. Like everything else in your life, you've chosen the easy way. Let others fight your battles. Pretended if you ignored something it would go away. You chose to hide behind excuses. That will not work now. You must confront your Talents and take control, or wither and die.

"Gods damn you, I don't know what to do. I

don't know how to control it. There's no one to teach me."

There is no one to do it for you, you must figure it out by yourself.

Hate is a harsh word, but right now I hate that little voice in my head more than—"Shit!"

The prickling tightness of power across my flesh burns, not the heat of a fever, or even a sunburn, but the intensity of an inferno. Terror and panic rip through my mind, coupling with my own paralyzing fear. Opening my eyes, I see grey wisps rise from my hands and feet, slowly crawling upward and inward. I gag and cough, as my last meal threatens to make an appearance. The urge to stop, drop and roll is squashed. I'm pretty sure that doesn't work if you're about to spontaneously combust.

Senses that disappeared during my internal disagreement return. Screams of pain, reverberate in my ears, making it down right impossible to tell the difference between those of others and my own. My nose is invaded by a burning scent I can't identify. Not flesh, not fiber, or even hair. Something worse.

Closing my eyes, I let what little control I have slip away to the mishmash of senses that aren't mine. The vomit-inducing flicker of a filmstrip out of control returns behind my eyelids. Several shadow entities gather around a single door as others rush to meet them. Some trying to push their way inside through the walls or doorway, only to be ejected. Others cower on the floor, contorted in pain and smoldering.

What would have the power to toss shadows around or cause them pain?

Wards. This is where Var and Vana have Einen. It has to be, it's the only explanation for the damage done to my shadows. A protective instinct rises deep within me. I need to help them. They are mine. How dare anyone harm what is mine? Yet another reason to hate those two.

Climbing to my feet, I let the sights and sounds of my mind's eye slip behind the rubble of my shields. Using the wall to keep my smoking body—never thought I'd get to say that, too bad it's literal and not figurative—upright, I push past the multiple layers of pain and panic, concentrating on what I've seen to lead me to my shadows and Einen.

Chapter 21

I'm tired of being mastered. I want to be the master. To do that, I have to crawl out of my comfort zone and let the power carry me, no matter what the consequences. Besides, I owe Einen. He saved me from drowning, now I get to save him from being grounded to his bedroom for eternity.

There's something very heady about intending to turn the tables on Var and Vana Royd. Gods or not, I'm going to flip their world upside-down. This feeling of… revenge? Hatred? Whatever it is, it drives me forward. Gives me the strength to cling to the wall and make my way down the never-ending hallway. Too bad it doesn't give me the brain power to figure out what I'm going to do when I reach my destination.

I take solace in the fact that I've learned to use the shadows to help me find my target. As messy and uncontrolled as it was, I did it, I found him. I may not have mastered my Talents, but I was able to use them. Now I have to use them again.

My gag reflex goes into overdrive as I round the last corner in Einen's maze of a mansion. The overspill sensation I felt is nothing compared to what I see and sense here. Shadows writhe on the floor, crying, moaning in pain and loss. The scent of burnt shadow *flesh* fills the air. And what can only be described as decay, not the sickly sweet smell of long dead flesh, but an empty, acrid scent burning the nostrils. Who would have thought shadows could die, or stink this much? It's not like you can smell them any other time.

Those that can, slither toward me, whimpering and shuddering with each movement. Whispered apologies ring in my ears. They have nothing to apologize for. This is on me for asking without thinking it through. This is on Var and Vana for thinking of only their own needs and wants.

The few still on their feet circle me, waiting for further instruction, but I have none to give. A part of me finds it appalling they would so easily toss away their lives because I asked. Another finds it heady. They truly are my minions. I command them, just as I commanded the dead. They would toss away everything to do as I ask. Cold fingers of guilt pull me back from the cliff above the fall into madness. I can't give into the heady feeling of dominance and superiority. I can't lose that glimmer of humanity so easily snuffed out by the temptation. I have a conscience and I intend on keeping it. I refuse to fall into the supposed schattenkind curse. I shake my head, looking at the fallen shadows who sacrificed themselves for me. What a waste. The only good to come of this is I learned a new skill, but it doesn't lessen the guilt. Shadows or not, they were alive and now they're dead, all due to my inexperience. I can't even help those still *alive*. I'm not a healer. Regenerating dead tissue might be my gig, but shadows aren't made of tissue. My hand slicing through one proves it, nothing, they're insubstantial. I have no idea how to *fix* something without substance. My best bet is to break Einen out and ask him. If anyone knows, it would be him.

Biting back my fear, I force my legs to take me to the door, a handful of shadow entities in tow. They look on in curiosity as I reach out, and piercing warnings ring out from those huddled on the floor.

"Hush, you've had your turn, now it's mine." Too many of them have been injured or killed, it's only fair that I give it a try. The wards make sense, they would have to withstand shadow magic or they wouldn't hold Einen. There has to be a way around them, because you can bet your bottom dollar Var and Vana have someone check on him. Hel, for all I know, they stop by periodically to gloat.

My fingers curl inward, unwilling to touch the door of their own accord. I'm so tired. The well of power is not bottomless as one would expect. You can only use it as fuel for so long before you crash, and I have no idea how much remains before I hit bottom. I have no idea what will happen if I hit that bottom. Will the shadows run amok? Will they dissolve into nothingness? Does what little control I have hold back more destructive things? If I crash will they escape?

"Stop overthinking and try and open the door. You're wasting energy."

One by one, I force my fingers to unfurl, hovering a hair's breadth from the door's surface. So far, so good, but I can feel energy radiating off the door. Not the bright warmth of summer sun that I've felt from Var's power, but something darker. Not the dark, cold emptiness of Hel's power, but something damn near sensual.

Amber. Musk. Need. Conquest. I slam the door on my senses, if I continue, sex will bury me alive. Without a doubt, the power belongs to Vana. Otherwise known as, Freya, goddess of sex, magic, and war. If you ask me, she's far more dangerous than any of the gods vying for my attention.

I felt her power once before, in a dream. Queen of the Valkyries, cloaked in leather and falcon feathers, morphing into the goddess of sex, adorned with amber and gold. The Brísingamen, the jewel whose power cannot be resisted. That damn necklace she always wears should have been a clue to her identity, but I wasn't thinking in terms of gods when I met her and her brother.

I can't figure out what this bitch has against

me, except I don't fall into her expectations of warrior or great beauty. Maybe if I fell into either of those categories, she wouldn't have a problem with the fascination her brother, Ric, and Teiran have with me. None of that matters right now. I need to focus on getting Einen released.

Taking a deep breath, I clamp my eyes shut, preparing to be tossed across the hall in a smoking heap. Cringing inward and outwardly, I use my body weight to force the contact, leaning forward until my hand presses against the door.

Chapter 22

Nothing. I'm still standing. Slowly, I open one eye. I'm not smoking, but a soft glow spreads out from under my hand. Varying colors swirling and dancing, like the watered-down glimpses of the Aurora Borealis, we get here in Iowa. Lucky me, I can touch the door as long as I'm capable of keeping my shields in place. I don't want to think about what will happen if they fail. The possibilities are endless.

Next trick, try the doorknob. Keeping contact, I slide my hand down and grasp the knob. Well, it's not locked in the conventional sense, but I already knew that, it turns, but does nothing. There's no physical lock keeping me from my goal, just Vana's wards.

Hel's realm, what now?

"Have you come back to torment me, Whore Queen?"

I can't help but smile. The words are a bit muffled, but that's definitely Einen's voice.

"Whore Queen? You used to call me Shadow Queen, have I been demoted?"

"Keely?"

"None other." My face hurts from the strain of my triumphant smile.

"How did you—

I'd accomplished what I'd set out to do, my shoulders sag and I relax, dropping my hand.

"Einen?" Nothing. "Damn it, what the hel happened?"

He's here, I'd just heard him, what changed? A breezy caress touches my shoulder and I turn to the shadow closest to me. It motions from my hand to the door and I quickly press my hand to the door again. Contact, I need to keep contact with the door.

"—trying to communicate with you and there was no response. Keely, are you still there?"

"Yeah, just figured out I have to keep touching the door to hear you. Now I need to figure out how to get you out of there. Any suggestions? I've already tried shadow magic." I glance at the fading figures on the floor, "That didn't work."

"You used your Talents?" There's a hint of pride in his voice, as well as, concern, and even a bit of anger.

"That's how I found you. I sent shadows to search the house, but when they tried to enter your room…"

"Of course they could not enter," he snaps. "That bitch whore shielded against any shadow magic to keep me inside. It was foolish of you to even try."

"Screw you, Einen. How the hel was I supposed to know that?"

"Forgive me, I did not think before I spoke." His words hold an edge that tempts me to take my hand off the door so I don't have to listen to the ungrateful twit. Maybe the others are right and I'm blinded by the persona he showed me as a child, or the need to have another like myself.

"Fine. Tell me what to do to get you out of there."

"You will need to retrieve the key from Freya."

Of course Vana would have the key. "Is it a literal key? A spell?"

A frustrated puff sounds from the other side, does he not realize I can hear him when he's that loud? I mean seriously, if you want help you shouldn't broadcast your irritation, at least have the decency to hide it until I'm gone.

"The key is an object."

"Your sarcasm isn't needed, Vereinen, especially if you want my help."

"Forgive me." Those words tumble from his lips so easily, they don't appear to mean much and I'm getting tired of them.

"Look, I know you're frustrated, but I'm not exactly having a picnic out here. I've been tossed into a shit storm and I'm coping the best I can. I don't see anyone else rushing to help you. I'm all you've got. You're just going to have to deal with me being inexperienced and uneducated when it comes to this crap."

"For—

"Don't say it, I don't want to hear those words again unless you really mean them. Now, back to where we left off, tell me about this key."

Chapter 23

I'm running on less than the required six hours of sleep and have expended most of my energy 'practicing' shadow stuff, at least that's what I tell the others. My little excursion pushed me light-years ahead of where I was with my Talents. The hows and whys are still a mystery, but it's a step in the right direction. They don't need to know I was hunting down Einen, or that I'm running on the shear adrenaline of finding him. The crash will come and it'll be explosive, but all I need to do is make it through the night. Bonus points, if make it through without loosing my temper.

"I need a touch-up, my roots are showing." Ms. Barker leans forward in my chair, holding her hair away from her face as she studies herself in the mirror.

Ms.—gods forbid you slip and call her Miss—Barker is a colleague of Var's attorney, Mark Jacobs. She's pushy, demanding, and over-achieving. Perfect qualities for a lawyer, but lousy for a client.

"Agreed, your *new growth* needs retouching." For crying out loud, people, the only way to see your roots is to pull out your hair. She'd have more problems than an unflattering style and a little grey if her *roots* where showing. One of these nights I'm going to demonstrate the procedure, but not tonight. The last thing I need is Ms. Barker to bitch to Mr. Jacobs, who will bitch to Var, who will bitch at me.

I gently direct her back into the chair and part her all-one-length hair at the crown. There's about a half-inch of virgin, light-brown showing, contrasting sharply with the jet-black of her chosen shade. "Would you like me to match your previous color?"

She turns and glares at me. "That's why I made the appointment."

The Morticia Addams look does her no favors. I would like nothing better than to strip the color back to something closer to her own shade and cut off at least five inches of nasty, over-processed ends. Maybe give her some bangs to camouflage her extremely high forehead and some layers to soften her sharp features. But from her response, there's no way she's going to let me change a hair on her head. I'll be lucky if she allows me to trim the ends.

Biting my tongue, I nod. She's a walk on eggshells type, so I phrase my questions carefully. "Did your stylist give you the formula for your color, or at least a brand?"

Her pinched lips nearly disappear with her

annoyance at my question. "The only reason I'm here is because it was strongly suggested by my superior."

Damn it, Var. It's bad enough he *suggests* his own employees throw their business my way, but to put the screws to people not directly under his employment, that's too much. And not the kind of clients I want in my chair.

"So you don't know what kind of color your usual stylist uses?"

Ms. Barker gives me a lemon-puckering look. "I just grab a box off the shelf."

Well, she's confirmed what I suspected. Home job. This explains the over processed shaft, instead of just retouching her new growth, she's been dumping the color all over. "Was this product just one bottle or did you have to mix two together?"

She holds up two fingers. I already know the answer, from the condition of her hair, but I needed confirmation. I can't stress enough how important it is that clients tell their stylist everything they do to their hair. Some chemicals don't play nice with each other, and without the correct steps the end result can be disastrous.

This job entails protective conditioner on the previously treated portion and careful placement of color to avoid over-lapping. And lots of watching. Thankfully, I don't have anything scheduled during her processing time.

I manage to match the color and even talk her into letting me cut off a hairstylist's inch. For most stylists, an inch means two, hence most people walking out missing an inch when they asked for a trim. If you want a true trim, ask for a wonder cut, as in I wonder if it was cut.

Leaving Ms. Barker at the desk, I grab a tube of reconstructive treatment off the retail shelf. "Here," I say, holding it out to her, "this is the treatment I was talking about."

She waves her hand. "I'll pass."

I can see from the look on her face as she signs the credit slip, she thinks she's already spent too much money. Grabbing her hand, I place the tube on her palm and wrap her fingers around it. "Trust me, it will make a difference."

Walking behind the desk, I grab a notepad and write the name of the product and salon use. Win nods, taking the pad. I think I broke Ms. Barker when I fixed her hair. The whole time she was in my chair she had two expressions, stern and sour. Now there's something else. Shock, maybe?

"Twice a week, twenty minutes," I say, before heading back to my vanity. As I turn the corner I hear her ask Win what I have open in six weeks. It's amazing what a little kindness will do, but to be honest, it's all part of a bigger picture. If she ends up coming back, I want her to trust me and her hair to be healthy. Maybe then she'll let me transform her from vampire groupie to polished lawyer. With any luck, I might even get her to smile.

Chapter 24

Leaning on the broom handle, Rey sighs. "I never thought I'd say this, but Keely, you've got to get your boss to stop sending so many referrals. I'm having a hel of a time fitting in my regulars."

"Yes," Dara says, wiping down her mirror. "Most of them do not wish to be here or expect some sort of special treatment."

"I had several ask for the Royd Enterprises discount and then got upset when I told them it didn't exist." Win's usual perky disposition disappeared when the last client left.

"You think that's bad?" Nyssa another towel in the laundry basket. "One of the men I was shampooing asked if *they* where real, then tried to bite them to find out."

"He tried to bite your boobs?" Rey's indignation speaks for us all. "Why didn't you say something?"

Nyssa shrugs. "I took care of it, he got a face full of something else."

"The man with the crew cut? The one that dripped all over my station?" asks Dara.

Nyssa nods, a wicked gleam lighting her eyes and a grin to match. "I wanted to keep going until he drowned, but didn't think management would approve."

"I would have helped you. I need his name, I'll be talking to Var tomorrow." After Nyssa's little revelation, I'm tempted to call him as soon as I get upstairs. It's a conversation that's been brewing, but I'm too damn tired to have it right now. With my coworkers or Var. "Anything else to add to the list of complaints?"

All four of them shake their heads.

"Okay, so I have lack of enthusiasm, no time to fit them in, demands for a discount, and boob biting."

"I think that pretty much sums it up," says Rey.

The others nod in agreement.

"I'll take care of it in the morning." I toss my towels into the basket Nyssa holds out to me. "I'll finish cleaning up later. See you guys tomorrow night."

"Keely, wait." Win rushes off to reception, returning with a manila envelope. "That geeky dude who was here the other night—you know, the one wearing the tweed suit—dropped this off for you."

Great, Mort the Tweed left me a package. "Thanks, Win." My own frown is mirrored on Dara's face. The rest of the crew looks on in curiosity, only to have it squashed when I slip the envelope under my arm. There's no way I'm opening this in front of anyone.

"See you all tomorrow night," I say, escaping before Dara can act on whatever is running through her mind.

The stairs are a challenge, but the need to be in my own space drives me. I can collapse once I'm locked inside my apartment. CC has positioned himself to be the first thing I see when entering. Par for the course, his needs come first. In this case, eating.

"Give me two seconds and I'll feed you." All I want to do is take my shoes off, but if I sit I won't get back up. Tossing the envelope on the couch, I head to the kitchen to fill my lord and master's bowl and check the fridge for something to drink.

Cat happily munching and soda in hand, I plop down next to the dreaded packet and glare at it as I slip off my shoes. Picking up the envelope, I attempt to weigh its contents. More than two or three pages, that's for sure. If I don't open the damn thing now, I'll dwell on all night. Then again, if I do open it, I'll be up all night thinking about it. This envelope and what it contains are a double edged sword and just as sharp.

A thin line of blood wells along the finger used to open the envelope. Setting everything down, I grab a tissue to staunch the blood. Why the hel do paper cuts hurt worse than when I slice my fingers with my shears? A sacrifice has been made to the gods of paper, so there better be something good in here.

Maybe my injury will get me out of training with my weapon of their choice. Using shears to cut hair is second nature, using my double-edged bodice shears to cut the flesh of others is awkward and distasteful. Keeping my bloody finger elevated, I aim for my lap as I dump the contents, but several sheets land on the couch and floor. I scramble to grab them before they become cat toys, succeeding in smearing blood on a few of them. The blood sacrifice is complete.

Finger rewrapped, I sort through the photocopies, until I find the accompanying letter of explanation.

Dear Miss Fey,

You seem hesitant to believe I can help you, maybe this will help you to make up your mind. I've enclosed copies from our files that you might find particularly interesting.

Mort

I glance over at CC. "Well, let's see what Mort thinks I will find particularly interesting."

Fifteen double-sided, no longer pristine, severely out of order sheets lay scattered over my coffee table and couch. From the questions and answers, it seems to be a transcript or interview, punctuated by some toe curling descriptions of how the answers were extracted. None of which will make a lick of sense until I get them back in order. Lucky for me someone numbered them.

The more I pick through the pages, the

deeper the feeling of dread digs its way into my core. Every question has something to do with the schattenkind. Every refusal to answer brings something painful to the interviewee. Whoever this poor sap was, he went through hel trying to keep his secrets. The person in charge of taking notes didn't skimp on the gory details, right down to when they brought in the vampire.

"Hel's Realm."

Mort had already warned me who'd given them info about Einen, but it took me reading three quarters of this dreadful thing to figure out it was Ric they'd tortured and eventually turned.

I'm pretty sure the female, who's name had been redacted, was Var's wife. I'd over heard Ric and Var discussing her, the Nazis, and what Ric had become. Why didn't they just ask her about Einen? Did she think her hubby was holding out on her?

It hadn't been the Ahnenerbe Society who'd done the damage, but they had asked the questions. They'd also come up with the idea of turning a liosâlfar into a vamp to see if he could withstand the sun, all in the name of science.

If good ol' Mort wanted me to believe they were the good guys, this didn't help his cause. Not to mention, there's not a damn thing here I didn't already know about Einen. It's just a horrible blow-by-blow of what happened to Ric and I didn't find it *particularly interesting* at all. Although, it did help me make up my mind about asking Mort for help.

Chapter 25

Sleep had not come easy and when I did fall asleep it was filled with nightmares spurred by unpleasant bedtime reading. I wake to my own screams—even though they were Ric's in my dream—and streaks of salty tears coating my face.

My fingers hurt, but aren't mangled and broken. The bathroom mirror reflects smooth, pale flesh on my back, no blood drenched, gaping wounds. Contrary to the lingering sensation of red-hot instruments, there are no marks along my extremities. And the only cut is the one on my finger, from last night's tangle with the envelope. The memory of the vampire attack is still so vivid, I even check my neck and eye teeth.

What Ric endured at the hands of the Ahnenerbe Society and Nazis makes my life look charmed. It's amazing how balanced he appears, I don't know if I'd be as accepting. Hel, I know my experiences in The Between and CU changed me, not to mention my first—and hopefully last—kill. I'd like to think what I've gone through made me a stronger person, but I have my doubts.

I have no idea how I'll face him with the weight

of this knowledge hanging over me. I can't fool myself into believing he won't notice the change in how I act around him. And there will be a change. I can't ignore or forget what I learned. I have no idea how he'll react to my knowing the gory details of his torture, but I do know he won't accept pity. The smart course of action is to talk to him, but not today. I'll add it to the growing list of distasteful things that must be done.

Today's distasteful act is a phone call to Var Royd, but first coffee. The scent and taste is a comforting normality in my less than normal life. With August's heat in full swing, I opt for a strong mix over ice—gotta love Teiran for turning me on to cold brewing—topped with a hearty splash of cream and a touch of sugary syrup as an extra treat. Coffee may not be magical enough to erase the distasteful things I have to do, but it helps soften the blow.

Picking up the dreaded cell phone, I scroll through the contact list and find what I assume is Var's private line. I should've used the speed dial, but keep forgetting. He's number one, it should be easy to remember, even though most days I consider him a big pile of number two.

Lovely, voicemail. And he gets pissed when I don't answer.

"Var, it's Keely, call me back. We need to talk." Wondering if I called about Haydn Koehler will light a fire under his ass faster than me mentioning it's about the salon.

Speaking of Mr. Koehler, I haven't even thought about my orders to spy on the thorn in Var's side. Eventually, Var's going to ask and I won't have a reason to sidestep that chat. I'd been able to find Einen using the shadows, can I repeat it with Haydn Koehler? But I'd been to Einen's house before, I have no idea where to find Koehler.

Truthfully, I'm not sure how I got to Einen's place. I wasn't asleep, so I wasn't dream walking. My body stayed in the apartment, so it couldn't have been border hopping. I'll have to give Annya a ring. If anyone can figure out what I'd done and how, it's my bestie. Daughter of a Sioux shaman and a Swedish witch or Völva—and follower of my *favorite* goddess, Freya a.k.a. Vana Royd— Annya's main Talent is dream walking and border hopping.

I suppose I start with finding out as much about my target as possible. Google is my friend and best resource, outside of following the guy around. And I've got some time between weapon's training and work to fill. What better way to fill it than playing on the internet in the name of research? Beats cleaning the apartment and salon.

Two hours and several iced lattes later, my mouse hand is cramped and a my head aches slightly from staring at the computer screen. I've perused the endless gossip sites and learned Haydn

Koehler's favorite food is tacos, he's into home brewing, has the average addiction to coffee—yay, something we can relate on, if I have to meet him— and is partial to raven-haired beauties. That leaves out any attempt at seduction or even attraction, I'm on the other end of the color spectrum. He went from reporter, to managing editor, finally ending up owning the Iowa Star, but still maintains the position of managing editor. Most of which I didn't know, not a big surprise since I rarely pay attention to the paper.

He's used his influence to terrorize Var Royd for years, be it in the editorial pages of the Star, or the monthly entertainment supplement. Basically, restaurant and entertainment reviews, mixed with gossip about the rich and famous of the Des Moines area. Makes me wonder why his involvement with the CFMT isn't called into question. I suppose reporters are put under the microscope of impartiality, but news paper owners don't have to worry about such things.

My research has left me with a pseudo plan. To do any type of spying, I have to see the interior of the Iowa Star. Once I get a basic layout, I'll be able to work the shadows. I didn't have to be in proximity at Einen's house, so it should be doable. I hope.

The cell vibrates along the surface of the desk, its screen flashing Var Royd's name. *Oh, yay, the fun begins.* I scramble to catch the dancing phone and slide my finger across the screen. "Yeah?"

"You called me, it should be me asking the questions." His voice is a smooth as milk chocolate and every bit as sweet, for the moment. "You said we need to talk, can I presume you have news about Haydn Koehler?"

"Thanks for returning my call, and no, this is about the salon."

"The salon is your problem."

"It's a problem you've caused."

"How, pray tell, did I cause a problem with your salon?"

"Your employees are the problem and you are the cause."

"Perhaps we should discuss this in person, when I have the time to spare. I am rather busy at the moment."

Great, the last thing I wanted was face time with him. "When? I need to get this settled as soon as possible."

"After you close for the evening, if it is acceptable to you."

"That won't be until around three."

"I shall arrive at three a.m., good-bye, Keely."

So not looking forward to ending my night with a visit from his lordship.

Chapter 26

This night can't get over fast enough, but I dread that last client walking out the door. I really, really don't want to deal with Var tonight. I'm tired, I'm bitchy, and I'm still freaked out by Mort's reading material. Ultimately, Var is to blame for what happened to Ric, but you can bet your bottom dollar he doesn't see it that way.

Not only does my body still feel sympathy pains, the crazy runes stitched into my arm itch like crazy. I know scar tissue can itch, but maybe wearing the Hel-blocking-bracelet twenty-four-seven isn't such a brilliant idea. Unless the itching is a sign she's trying to get ahold of me, then better on than off. The last time she tried to make a point, it felt like she lit the mark on fire. I'm sure she has something much worse planed for when I do contact her. So why not put that meeting off as long as possible?

From working for them to being marked by them, I am so sick of dealing with gods. Thanks to Einen, I now have to steal from one. Too bad he didn't see exactly what form this *key* takes, add it to the list of things I need to figure out on my own. Damn, that list is getting ridiculously long. At least I know there is a physical key, even if it's not a typical door key. Now all I have to do is figure what it is and where she keeps it. Is it hidden in her house? Does she keep it on her?

That necklace—which I assume is Brísingamen—is the only thing she constantly wears. There is no way she'd use that as a vessel. She can't be that stupid, but a girl can dream. It would be like killing two birds with one amber stone. I could let Einen out and have something to hold over her. Stealing what I assume is a source of power is also much more dangerous and I'm hardly an experienced cat burglar.

Nobody said adulthood would be easy, but right now I'd rather go back and relive my hellish high school years. Then again, there isn't much difference between then and what I'm going through now. Thanks to the block on my Talents expiring, I'm going through Enchant puberty and dealing with gods is reminiscent of the typical high school cliques. There's a whole lot of backstabbing, gossiping, and the usual race to the top of the popularity list. The big difference is having the cute, popular boys show more than a passing interest in me. Can't say I'm not enjoying that turn in events.

I know it's not really me they want, it has more to do with what I am. In Var's case, wanting to use my Talent to further his advantage in the game he's playing. With Ric and Teiran, it has something to do with species attraction, an elf thing, I guess. And the connection between Einen and I is similar, with the added pull of both of us being schattenkind. Regardless of the reason, it's nice to be considered attractive, especially when you're more than double your twenties.

Soft ambient music switched to a thundering base and harsher tone. The Cult, I think. Dara must be in control of the night's cleaning music. Win unlocks the door when the band hits the chorus of Sun King, letting in Var Royd. Talk about timing, not that Var knows this is the ringtone Rey used for him on my phone. Rey *graciously* programed special ringtones for all my contacts, setting his own as The Fox. According to him, the fox says anything he damn well pleases.

From the look on Var's face, this conversation is not going to go well. I'd place bets that the last thing he wanted to do this evening is drive to The Meadows and chat about what he considers my problem. Tough, it's a problem he created and he's going to have to fix it.

"Thanks for coming, Var."

"Keely," he says tartly, scanning the room.

Everyone pretends to concentrate on cleaning, except Dara. She does that whole lean-against-the-vanity-polishing-her-shears bit. I've been on the receiving end of that glare and it's not pleasant.

It doesn't faze Var, he seems to be enjoying their battle of 'who's got the bigger balls.' He actually smiles at her. It's really more of a showing of teeth than a true smile, baiting her to do something. She pulls away from the vanity, standing straight, her hand clenched around the shears as if they are weapon of destruction instead of creation.

I grab his arm, directing him away from her. The last thing we need is a bigger mess to cleanup, one that would shut us down for repairs. "Let's go in the break room so we can chat."

"I would rather we take this somewhere more private, your apartment, perhaps?" The stormy swirl in his eyes tells me we're going to be discussing more than just my salon.

"Yeah, that'll work." I turn, facing a room filled with caution, curiosity, and a teensy bit of pity. I appreciate their concern, but Var is my problem, not theirs. I said I'd fix our clientele problem and I will. It's part of being the boss. "Don't forget to lock up when you leave, see you all tomorrow."

The long trudge up stairs to my place isn't long enough with my guest tagging along. Thankfully, he's less talkative than usual, allowing me to concentrate on how to present my list of complaints. Too many people, not enough time. No discount for Royd Enterprises employees. And most important of all, no sexual comments or boob biting.

Per usual, there's a hungry cat waiting behind door number one. CC and Var have a stare down while I fill the food dish. It ends with the cat hissing and backing away when Var leans down to pet him.

"Touchy creature, isn't she?"

"She's a he, and yes, it takes him some time to warm up to people. Can I get you something to drink? Coffee? Tea? A soda?" I would offer wine or beer, but I don't want our meeting to be confused with a social gathering.

"A glass of water would be nice."

"Bottled or tap?"

"Bottled if you have some."

Of course I have some, I wouldn't have offered if I didn't. Luckily, auto respond's shut off. Opening the fridge, I grab a bottle of water and a soda. "Do you need a glass?"

"A glass is not necessary." But preferred his tone says, so I grab a glass and fill it before handing it to him.

I motion toward an armchair as I take up residence on the couch. "Thanks for coming. There are a couple of things I need to talk to you about concerning your employees."

He raises a brow. "What have the Sword and Shield done?"

"Not them, your other employees. The ones you keep sending to the salon."

"You dislike the extra income?"

"Not at all, it's more along the lines of their… behavior."

"How so?"

"First off, we don't have a discount for them, never have and never will." I take his nodding as a good sign. "Second, it's not that we don't appreciate the business, but clients who don't want to be here, shouldn't be forced."

"I only suggested they frequent your establishment."

"Understood, but please let them know they don't have to. Last, but not least, sexual misconduct is not tolerated."

"Sexual misconduct?"

"One of your male employees took it upon himself to… complement Nyssa's figure."

"The nixie is very attractive."

"And endowed, we know, but it doesn't mean he can ask personal questions, or use his teeth to find out if they are real."

Var's lips compress into a thin line. "It will not happen again."

"Thank you."

"Now I have a question for you."

Here it comes, the real reason he's here, Haydn Koehler.

"How long?"

Chapter 27

The look in his eyes and his tone make me wish I hadn't agreed to meet up here, alone. "How long what?"

Var is on me before I can blink. Seizing my arm, he jerks me to my feet. "How long"—his words coming from behind clenched teeth—"have you been meeting with him?"

"Let go, Var, you're hurting me."

"How long?"

I'm trapped between him, the couch, and the coffee table. No where to go but back, or over the furniture. Not that I'd get very far with him hanging on to my arm.

"How long have you been meeting with him?"

"Look, I'm not into mind games so if you have something to say, say it."

"I asked you a question."

"And I don't understand it, so elaborate if you want an answer." I think I understand, but admitting it would put the ball in his court and I kind of like keeping him off balance. Vereinen is not a subject up for discussion with anyone, let alone one of the people who banished him. There's no way in hel, I'm confessing to having found him.

"That abomination"—disgust twists that handsome face—"I know you have been with him, I can smell the stench of shadow on you."

"Stench of shadow? Could it be me you smell?"

His grip on my arm tightens as he yanks me toward him. "You smell of guilt," he whispers between clenched teeth and leans in closer, his other hand snaking up between us. "Guilt and fear." His fingers clamp onto my nipple and give it a twist, nearly bringing me to my knees, but his other hand keeps me upright.

"First, I don't know what you're talking about. Second, I haven't had time to shower, so stop telling me I stink." It's a fight to keep my voice at a normal tone, when the pain urges it to a higher octave. What the hel, does he seriously think manhandling my lady parts is going to make me talk?

"Tell me how you found him." The pressure of his fingers increases.

Nails bite into my palm, I refuse to give him the satisfaction of admitting it hurts. I so want to lift my knee upward, but something tells me it would only make things worse. "I don't know what you're talking about."

This time he gives my nipple a vicious twist. Does he think he's going to unscrew it? Part of me feels the urge to grab something on him, but

I'm afraid he'd take it as an invitation. "Yes, you do. Tell me how you found him."

"I haven't found anything, or anyone."

Leaning in, his lips brush against my ear, "That thing cannot give you what I can. You seem to forget I own you."

I laugh, partly fear and partly just to be mean. "It might surprise you to know, I don't want anything from you."

His head snaps back and he stares me in the eye. An emotion other than anger and accusation flashes across his face. Confusion? Now that would make my day, I confused the great and powerful, Var Royd. As fleeting as everything else in my life, the look is gone.

"And you may own my business and home, but not me. Working for you doesn't make me your property."

Tightness shimmies across my skin and from the look on his face, I know my eyes are turning a lovely, endless black. No pupil, no iris, no white, just solid black, a physical sign that I'm powering up. His fingers release and his hands drop to his sides. I feel my lips stretch into a smile, obviously not attractive or inviting, as he takes a step back. So, there are some kickbacks to having this Talent. It's about time I find something positive, but I need to reel it in, because I can feel it pulling me in every direction.

It feels like I took a wrecking ball to the head. My lovely brick wall shudders. The grittiness of brick dust coats my throat and mouth. I have no idea how long I can hold on before everything comes tumbling down. That would kind of screw up the whole *yay, me* moment. Closing my eyes I see a shadowy figure between me and the crumbling wall, pushing loose bricks back into place. The quaking slowly dissipates to a slight tremble and the figure is gone. I don't have time to wonder if it was Einen, Hel, or my imagination. I'm just thankful.

Taking a deep breath, I open them again and stare my opponent down with feigned confidence. With one last nasty look, he stalks off slamming the door behind him. The vase on the stand next to it topples to the floor, becoming a mess of shattered glass, foliage, and water.

The child in me wants to scream, fuck you, but I hold it in. Not exactly classy after I'd won that little power play. I also resist pressing a hand to my throbbing breast. It's not the time to show weakness either even if no one is there to see me. Good practice for the next time, and there will be a next time. It's inevitable that we'll butt heads again.

"Fuckin' power games," I say, moving through the kitchen. That's all that was, he doesn't know I found Einen, he was testing the water. Something must have tipped him or his bitch of a sister off.

Freakin' Einen better have not been tooting his horn about how he's going to escape. His butt, I'm not afraid to kick.

Plain soda is not going to do it, I search the cupboard for that bottle of whiskey I have stashed away. To hel with the soda, or a glass, I tip the bottle to my lips and take a large gulp. Go out to dinner with the guy and he thinks he owns you. Agree to work for the guy and he thinks he owns you. Can't imagine what it would be like if I'd actually had sex with him. I know it's my own fault. I signed on as his Shadow and that opened the door. That he holds the note on my home and business doesn't help the situation. If it comes down to it, he can keep the building. I'll find someplace else to live and work. Who am I lying to? He'll never let me go, I'm too important to his power base.

I take another swig. Alcohol is probably not a good idea for many reasons. Anger and uncontrolled Talents being two, but I don't care. Fear would be another, but I'll worry about that later. It's not the first and it won't be the last time I do something I shouldn't.

Chapter 28

"Again. This time at least make it *look* like you are trying." Teiran's exasperation is all too evident.

"I *am* trying."

"Then try harder and pay attention to your opponent, not whether or not you have broken a nail."

That's it, I've had it with the you're-being-too-girly insults. He wouldn't treat Dara this way. Then again, Dara would probably side with him. Lucky for me, she can't join us when the sun is up. If I'm a little hesitant with my sparing partner today, it has nothing to do with being a girl and everything to do with what I learned about Ric. Beating on a guy—not that I probably do much, if any, damage—who's endured such horrors doesn't sit well with me. I know it has no bearing on what we're doing, but I can't scrub the mental pictures of what happened to him from my brain. It's a problem I need to get past in my own way, without letting him know. I'm not ready for that conversation.

"I'm done." Putting my shears back into the sheath, that now hangs from a nifty belt Ric and

Teiran gave me, I plunk down on the weight bench. One of the few places to sit—besides the floor—in Teiran's *workout* room. Technically, it's his basement, but right now it feels more like a torture chamber in a dungeon. It's the only room in his house that I know inside and out. I didn't even get the grand tour when we started training here. We come in and go right down the stairs. Although, to be fair, he did show me where the bathroom is located. The one in the—you guessed it—basement.

"I said, again." The words are forced from between clenched teeth. I wonder if Var's employee health plan covers dental. Oh, that's right, according to Haydn Koehler and the CFMT, Royd Enterprises doesn't cover Ens. They might be right, I haven't heard a word about employee coverage.

"And I said, I'm done." From tumbling on the mat to degrees of damage achieved by stabbing certain body parts, I've had enough roughhousing with Ric and Teiran for one day. "It's pushing four o'clock and I need a break before work."

Teiran runs his hands through his hair and stares at me as if I'm the laziest thing he's ever seen. I'd like to see him balance two jobs, defense training, practicing new Talents, and having a life. What the hel am I saying? I don't have a life outside things pertaining to one job or the other.

Ric moves to stand beside me and places a hand on my shoulder. "She is right, Teiran, it's late and she has to work tonight."

Ignoring the growly beast in the center of the room, I shoot my sparring partner a smile. He's really working on his vernacular, and I applaud his attempts to move into a more current century. I also appreciate Ric's more gentle—although, he calls it strategic or psychological—method of teaching. He believes I need to know the why as well as the how of physical combat. Unlike Teiran, who's all about pounding your opponent into the ground. I swear, he gets some sort of perverse pleasure from kicking the crap out of me, all in the name of 'learning' of course. They are so different in so many ways. From physical traits to how they perceive the world and their place in it, maybe that's why they complement each other so well.

I gather up my stuff and head for the stairs, intent on getting out the door and into my car before something comes along to stop me. "Thanks for the rough and tumble, boys, meet you back here at the wolf cave tomorrow."

Having to sprint up the stairs after the wolf comment is painful, but so worth it. Hel, calling them boys probably got a rise out of him too. I can't resist doing little things to irritate Teiran, no matter how high schoolish. Just because society deems anyone past their twenties is old, it doesn't mean you can't act like a kid when you get the chance. I intend on taking every chance I can, including putting the top down on the 'Stang and not apologizing to the residents of The Meadows and surrounding area for cranking the music.

Even at a year younger than I am, the '69 muscle car with its antique technology refuses to be considered old. If nothing else it screams badassery, something I wish would rub off on me. It doesn't matter how much 'training' I do, I doubt I will ever reach that level of being a badass. At least not full-time. If I'm using my Talents it's there in spades, but once I stop it wears off. Maybe it has something to do with confidence, all of my 'teachers' have more than their fair share. I'm more than confident behind the chair, but on the mat, I'm a fumbling novice. On the other hand, my 'teachers' have been doing this way longer than I've been alive. With thousands of years of training they'll always be better than I am. Suddenly, I don't feel so bad.

It's amazing how driving on dirt and gravel slows down what should only be a fifteen minute drive. Bumpy country roads are not conducive to speed, and you never know when wildlife will pop out. I love my car too much to ignore the conditions, no matter how much I want to get home and squeeze in a little shadow practice before work.

With Google playing the part of my best friend, I've gathered several pictures and a basic layout of Haydn Kohler's office. If I keep digging, I might even find a few pictures of his house, but I'd need interior shots. Those are harder to find and exploring his business is safer than attempting his home. He's not a stupid man and more than likely has wards guarding his personal space against intruders. The last thing I need is my shadow spies triggering them. Kinda defeats the spying part when you get caught.

Speaking of spies, the trees and sky are thick with mourning doves.

Chapter 29

Frickin' Hel, why can't she take a hint? I can only deal with one god at a time and right now I'm focused on making nice with Var. After our last meeting, I need to give him something on Kohler. I'd rather his focus shift from his suspicions of my finding Einen to my digging up dirt on his nemesis. Gods seem to suffer from *look, squirrel!* syndrome. If I can dangle something sparkly in front of him, he'll back off on the Einen subject.

Damn it. Seeing Mort leaning against the wall next to my door, I'm tempted to keep driving. So tempted. I don't, but I do bitch about it. Pulling into the garage, I see him following in the rearview mirror and bitch some more.

"What do you want, Mort?" I ask, securing the garage, before turning to face the newest pain in my ass.

"Did you get my package, Miss Fey?"

"Yep." Putting my back against the garage—see, I did learn something from my defense training, never leave your back exposed—I cross my arms and wait for him to elaborate.

"Did you read the contents?"

I sigh, fighting to keep from rolling my eyes. Does he seriously think I wouldn't look at what he gave me? "Just get to the point, Mort."

He shuffles his feet, puts his hands in his pockets, removes them, then puts them back. I stop him before he can repeat the action again. "I don't have time to play games with you. Get. To. The. Point."

"Did it prove I know what you are and can help you?"

"No, it disgusted me. I have no idea why you would think something like that would *help* me. If it did anything I proved what assholes the Nazis were."

"I told you, I'm not a Nazi."

"You keep saying that, but sending me a transcript detailing the torture of one of my friends sure doesn't prove it."

"It proves he's not your friend." His voice raises and he takes a step forward.

I standup straight, my hand dropping to rest on the shears hanging at my hip—my trainers insist I wear at all times, to get used to them—not sure if it's passion or aggression driving him. If it's aggression, I hope I remember enough of my training to disable him.

His gaze lands on the weapon strapped to my waist, his Adam's apple rises and falls as he stops in his tracks. The possibility of me using my Talents fascinates him, but a physical weapon scares him. Something to keep in mind.

"Alric Brand is not your friend, he sold-out the other schattenkind and he'll do the same to you."

"Anyone can be *convinced* to sell someone out when faced with the barbarity of that kind of torment." I have to fight the shiver of repulsion brought on by the mental pictures of what Ric endured.

"I didn't say I agreed with their methods—"

"I don't care if you agreed or not, it was repulsive and I didn't need to see that shit. None of it was helpful at all." It did give me an insight into how Ric became a vamp, but Mort doesn't need to know that.

His chin rests against his chest. "I'm sorry, I didn't realize it would upset you."

Is he stupid, or is his social awkwardness more than just an appearance? No matter how sorry he looks, I refuse to brush it off by giving him an empty 'it's alright' because it's *not* alright. The boy needs to learn reactions are not always going to be what he expects. There's something wrong with anyone who isn't upset, to some degree, by reading crap like that. I don't think Mort's a psychopath, but there is something off with the social behavior portion of his character.

"Is that why you're here? To check up on my late night reading?"

"No, not really, I'm hoping you'll grab a cup of coffee with me and discuss your physiology."

"My physiology? Is that the technical way of saying you want to discuss my Talents?"

Nodding vigorously, his expression brightens. "Yes, I'd like to chat about schattenkinds and what you can do."

"Has anyone told you, you have an abnormal obsession with shadows?"

"Oh, it's not just shadows, there are many things you're capable of manipulating."

"The whole necromancer thing."

"You are so much more than a simple necromancer."

"From what I hear, there's nothing simple about necromancy."

He chuckles. "Forgive me, you are quite right. Necromancy is not simple, but what you are capable of is far more complex."

"What I'm capable of?"

The smile stays, but the hardened look in his eyes makes me rethink my thoughts on him not being a psycho. "Don't pretend ignorance, I'm not foolish enough to believe you don't know what I'm talking about."

I shrug, hoping to keep the creeping fear pushed down, hidden. "So what do you think I am, if I'm not a simple necromancer?"

"There's no word or classification for what

you are, well, because there are only two of you in existence. Necromancy is the practice of communicating with the dead. To be a necromancer is to divine the future by this communication. They do not manipulate them, nor bend them to their will. The title has been bastardized through the years, the true meaning lost. You're more than that."

"Uh-huh." Interesting, I'm not a necromancer in the dictionary sense. So what am I? "Go on."

Keeping him on topic and asking questions definitely makes the boy happy. "Perhaps we should finish our discussion over at Midnite Expresso."

"No, this isn't a conversation for public consumption."

"Then your apartment?"

There is absolutely no way, Mort the Tweed is getting inside my personal space. I shake my head. "Whatever you have to say, say it fast, I've got things to do."

He looks a little crestfallen, but it passes as quickly as it appeared, when he opens his mouth. "Vampires believe you to be a *true* necromancer because of your control over them, but by definition there is no such thing. In reality a necromancer, true or not, cannot control the dead, not the way you can."

Glancing at the clock on my phone, I wave my hand trying to speed him along. He's starting to repeat himself. "Necromancers commune with, but don't control the dead. Got it."

"Necrokinesis would be a better term to describe what you do, it's the manipulation of death and dead energy. Controlling anything that is dead with by sheer will, rather than having to use magic. Although, being an Enchant you are magic by birth."

"So you're saying an Un could do what I do by using magic, like charms or spells?"

"I supposed it would be possible if the charm or spell is powerful enough, but I haven't come across any documented cases."

"How about your Nazi buddies, any of them try?"

His cheeks grow red and it's not from standing in the sun. "I told you, I'm not a Nazi. But yes, they tried, and failed."

"Leading to the *study* of *my* kind."

"Yes."

Dickheads were probably going to weaponize us like they tried to do with Ric. "And this necrokinesis is why the vamps are so scared of us?"

He shakes his head. "My predecessors came to the conclusion it's because of what you are—half dark, half light—that gives you the ability to control beings existing in a half state. Vampires, for example. They are neither dead, nor alive, and that is why they fear you."

Makes sense. I've now got enough to do research on my own. If they boy had been thinking, he wouldn't have told me so much at once. I glance at the time again and fiddle with my keys. "As interesting as all this has been, I've got to cut you off here, Mort."

"When can we meet again? I have more to tell you and think I could be helpful in learning to harness your Talents."

"Don't call me, I'll call you." Hurrying toward my building, I ignore his protests over the lack of my number. That is one person who will never get my number. The eagerness of his expression—and questionable mental state—has me wondering about susceptibility to Faery Fever. Is he infatuated with Enchants, or is he only interested in what he claims? Could there be a more nefarious reason?

Chapter 30

If Mort has Faery Fever, it might explain his infatuation with my Talents. Usually, when an Unchant is infected with the Fever, they obsess over becoming an Enchant, but it's not possible. Even The Collector, with his stolen Talent amulet—I hope that thing is lost forever—wouldn't have been considered an Enchant. Stanley-The Collector-Lewis would have remained an Un, with a magical necklace that helped him emulate En Talent. If you aren't born with magic, you'll never be magical.

All of us *mythical creatures* were born the way we are, with the exception of vampires. Technically, vamps aren't Ens. They might have been before they were turned, but turning an Un doesn't guarantee them magical powers, and there's no guarantee an En will keep their Talent once turned, or if it will manifest in some other way.

Speaking of Talent, I have about an hour to practice mine before I have to get ready for work. With a quick stop to turn on the computer, I jump in the shower, a must after a workout with the boys. Too bad it wasn't a different type of workout. With teachers like mine, it's all I can do to keep from getting too distracted during my lessons. Anger—with myself for not picking up the techniques quicker, and at Teiran for being such a hard-ass—is my crutch when it comes to shaking off the naughty thoughts. Cold showers after a go around don't hurt, nothing like washing off the stink and freezing the desire. Talk about multi-tasking.

While my hair dries, I pull up pictures of the Iowa Star. Thank you, interwebs, for giving me a remote look into the place I need to infiltrate. I'm not sure if I can send in the shadows, so to speak, from this distance or without seeing the place first hand. Who knows how old these photos are. They might have remodeled or moved furnishings. One small change, like moving a chair, would leave me high and dry. No chair, no shadow. No shadow, no info. No info equals a pissed off boss. With as many times as I've pissed him off lately, I don't want to experience the repercussions. You can bet there are repercussions, my nipple aches just thinking about them, and not in a good way.

Scrolling through the pictures, I decide on what I'm guessing is reception. There are a ton of pictures, ranging from candid to promotional, and they're probably the most recent taken. A big desk is the centerpiece of the room, along with a scattering of chairs and end tables. Any of the furnishings would work, but I chose to focus on the desk. The artificial lighting is a bonus, I won't have to rely on guessing what time of day the picture was taken and if it correlates with the current time.

What I'm about to do would be easier if I could reliably border hop. Problem is, I've never done it intentionally, I have no idea how it happened. My trip to Hel's place had coincided with The Collector pounding my head against a cave floor while I wished myself somewhere else. Granted, he'd breached the veil, I suppose that made it easier to travel between realms. I'm not certain my trips to see Einen were actual physical visits, no matter how *physical* they felt. I'm leaning more toward them being all in my head, more akin to dream walking. I don't even know if it's possible to use border hopping to enter buildings on the same plane. If it is how do I know I won't materialize in a cluster of people?

Quizzing Annya would be the smart thing to do, my bff is the queen of dream walking and can border hop like nobody's business, but who says I'm smart? I certainly never have. Considering the recent shit decisions I've made, I might even be the stupidest person alive.

Having studied several pictures from every angle possible, I set a timer to keep me on schedule. It doesn't look good if the boss is late for work, not to mention, falling behind on a busy night sucks. I close my eyes, concentrating on placing myself into the room. With the pictures as my guide, I begin to explore. Once I'm comfortable, or as comfortable as I can be with my cloak and dagger intentions, I switch up my focus to the shadows stretching out from the ginormous desk.

"Shadows are my friends," I tell myself, loosening the hold on my mental shields. I open that part of me that knows them intimately. Slowly, I pace through the shadows of the room, conjured in my mind by the photos. The soft whisper of touch across my skin. The coolness, I know they hold, flowing over me. The sounds. Yes, shadows make noise. The average person would probably consider them a trick of the mind. Unexplained noises categorized under old houses creak, or it was the wind. For me it's different, they speak to me, not necessarily in words, more like impressions and emotions, giving them the semblance of being flesh and bone. Probably similar to what Ric *heard*, before becoming a vamp opened his Talent to receiving words.

They can also act as my eyes, proven by my search of Einen's house. A stomach lurching, rollercoaster ride I'm not sure I want to repeat. Supposedly, they'll also act as a speaker, allowing me to hear the things around them. Something I haven't experienced firsthand, all I have to go on is Var's insistence it's another tool in my arsenal. One I better learn to use, like yesterday.

I try to experience the actual space, but all I see is the static room depicted in the photos. No life, no movement, even the receptionist behind the desk stays picture perfect still. I try and listen, but all I hear are the normal sounds of my apartment, the street below, and then a loud beeping that rips my concentration from the room.

All indications I've failed to reach my target.

Chapter 31

I pull into the parking garage, cranky and tired. I'm skimping on sleep, not something I recommend, but with so much on my plate I have to make sacrifices. Can't cut my work hours, I have bills to pay. Can't skip training, Rick and Teiran would have a cow. Can't ignore Var's orders, heavens know what he'd do to me. I've already given up any sort of a personal life, leaving sleep as the only thing left. So here I am, in downtown Des Moines, at what I would consider the butt-crack of dawn. Eight thirty a.m., to be exact.

With yesterday's discovery that pictures aren't precise enough, I intend on personally visiting the Iowa Star. I had planned to hang out in reception, but quickly wrote that off. A strange woman loitering around the office and no one asks questions? Highly unlikely. Also unlikely, me wandering around pretending I work there. I'd kidded myself into thinking I could pose as a cleaning woman. Chances they'd have the cleaning staff there during the day? Zero to none. Then there was the, "Can I use your restroom?" ploy. If hanging out in reception wasn't questionable enough, hanging in a bathroom… well, lack of sleep gives you all kinds of impossible and stupid scenarios.

My new, and possibly perfect plan, entails joining a college tour. The internet is a wonderful tool, and led me to Des Moines Community College's site. The DMACC journalism class is taking a tour of the Star today and I'm going along. That's right, middle-aged, Keely Fey is going to pretend to be a college student. Thank the gods so many old folks, like myself, are going back to school these days. When I was of age to attend, someone as old as I am would have stuck out like a sore thumb.

Thanks to my elven—maybe it's my upbringing or the fact that I'm American, but elf slips off the tongue easier than âlfar—heritage, I look younger than my middle years. I can probably pass for late twenties, early thirties with the right clothing and makeup. And that's what I'm attempting today.

No one questions the bookish brunette slipping into the group as they enter the newspaper's building, thanks to a quick cut-and-color, a pair of thick-framed glasses, and a lot of body makeup applied to my visible skin to give it a 'normal' tone, instead of my usual pale, greyish white. The makeup will wash off, and the head can be shaved and regrown before my shift tonight. It's the ultimate disguise to go along with the ultimate plan.

That is, until I hear the tour guide ask to see college IDs. Damn it!

My stomach flutters and muscles twitch as my brain screams *flee*, but I'm surrounded by students digging in pockets and bags for their identification. I'm jostled from left to right, back to front. The oversized book bag draped over my shoulder swings, smacking the surge of bodies, and the prop notebook slips from my fingers, falling under shuffling feet. Crouching to retrieve it, I have a total Velma moment. My glasses are knocked from my face and I'm left crawling around between flip-flops and tennis shoes. A pair of stylish pumps emerge from the sea of comfy footwear. Weaseling my way past them, a couple of helpful hands pull me to my feet, another set hands me my Clark Kent disguise. Brushing off questions of concern, I slip further into the group.

Once everyone has passed inspection, our tour guide introduces herself as Betty, although she gives off more of a Veronica vibe. She's practical to the point of bitchiness, and definitely not in the mood to be escorting a group of collage students when she has better things to do, whatever they may be. She doesn't look like a reporter, but I do recognize a few familiar faces from when I was suspected of being The Collector. Here's hoping none of them are savvy enough to recognize me.

As Betty prattles on about the inner workings

of a newspaper, I study my surroundings. Plenty of things casting shadows, desks, file cabinets, and of course a water cooler in the main area. I could use any of those to spy on the underlings, but the head honcho's office holds my interest. Wonder if that's included in the tour? Doesn't matter, I'm gonna see it anyway.

I slow down, letting the group flow around me until I'm alone in my search. Haydn Kohler's office isn't hard to find, but it does surprise me. His name is emblazoned on a gold placard on a half open door closer to the hubbub. I give it a tap with my elbow, figuring if I hear anything I can slip off without being seen. When no sound comes from the room, I stick my head in. Nobody around, my lucky day.

I check to see if anyone is paying attention before I step inside a room slightly bigger than my second bedroom. You'd think the newspaper's owner would have the big office, not the broom closet, or at least a window. Not that that's bad. Matter of fact, the room's size, along with the spareness of furnishing, makes it easier on me. There are two file cabinets, a couple of chairs, a fake palm in the corner behind a large leather executive chair, and desk that dominates the room. Haydn must be a big man to need the big chair and desk. I wonder how they got it in here. The last thing I check is the lighting, florescent like everything else and a small desk light. Checking behind the fake plant, I find an uplight. How convenient. Tiny slivers of shadow, cast by the thin palm leaves, will be easier to control and less noticeable. Probably the best vantage point for my shadowy spies.

Chapter 32

Heart pounding, I sit in my car contemplating my nearly-botched mission. Exiting wasn't any easier than entering. It was worse and getting caught coming out of the boss's office didn't help. I covered with the bathroom excuse. Why does everyone fall for that? Faking stomach problems must be the key, no one wants to be a part of whatever is trying to evacuate your insides. After a quick trip into the *correct* room, I make it to the door, but not outside. Instead, I end up doing the do-si-do door dance with the object of my surveillance. And yes, his size does warrant the jumbo chair and desk. He didn't give me more than a moment's notice. We shared a quick laugh and apologies on both sides before I was able to extract myself from the building.

If I have faery godmother or guardian angel, they must be on vacation, like permanently, or they just pick and chose when they want to help.

On the bright side, I completed what I came to do, and Haydn Kohler is where I need him. Fingers crossed he'll be in his office soon. Now all I have to do is call up the shadows and hope location works like cell towers. The closer you are, the better the connection. Easy peasy, right?

Unlike other public venues, the parking garage gives me a finite amount of privacy. The only prying eyes are the security cameras, but all they'll see is a woman hanging out in her car. If I can keep myself in check that's all they see. Should've brought a book and bag lunch to complete my disguise, but considering it's only quarter to ten, lunch break wouldn't be believable. And I'm all about the believable. Not. Much of my life has become unbelievable.

I'm tempted to put the top down on the car, instead of sitting here melting in the August heat, but brainless here forgot to check the location of the cameras. What if they see my face? I'd been smart enough to keep my head down exiting and entering. Keeping the top up will make it harder to see more than a chick with short dark hair sitting in a car.

Shit, what if they use my car or license plate, put two and two together, and figure out it's Var's Shadow spying? Should I have obscured my license plate or, better yet, borrowed a car? Too late now.

"Hel's Realm, get a handle on yourself, Keely. You're over thinking, Des Moines Iowa doesn't have Hollywood technology."

It's amazing the crap that goes through my mind, but I'm an over-thinker, or paranoid, or both. But wouldn't it be cool if it was just like the movies? Our cool, calm, and collected heroine sneaks into enemy territory and snags the coveted item right from under the bad guy's nose, complete with awesome background music.

Unfortunately, I'm dealing with real life and have to put away the fears, doubts, and fantasies, or channel them into what I'm about to attempt. Fear's upside triggers my Talent, but there's a downside too. It forces my Talents into self-preservation mode, making them difficult, sometimes downright impossible, to control.

Even with my handful of mildly successful attempts, I'm not so full of myself to forget it can all go south in a fraction of a second. But maybe I can channel some of that fantasy into confidence and control them.

I've done this before and can do it again, even though the circumstances are slightly different. I need to stop *thinking* and start *doing*. Maybe a little music will settle my nerves. Non-caffeine-induced jitters shake my hand as I shove the phone charger into the cigarette lighter. I'm still mistrustful of the battery life claims, no matter how many times everyone assures me I have nothing to worry about.

Scrolling through the songs Rey loaded into the music player, I can't seem to find the *right* song. There are some of the usual suspects, but he's also loaded a ton of music that will, as he puts it, "transition me into the current decade." My finger hovers over a Duran Duran tune, but bumps Pat Benatar's Shadows of the Night. Guess it's fitting, it may not be night, but I'm still *running* with the shadows.

The speaker on the phone isn't the best way to listen, but I don't dare use the earbuds. It's going to be hard enough splitting my focus between the shadows in the office and my surroundings. Last thing I need is some nosey security guard sneaking up on me while I'm concentrating. The repercussions could be devastating, not only to my mission, but to anyone in that building and possibly this parking garage. I don't need any more blood on my hands. Taking one life weighs as heavily on my conscience as the sticky August air weighing down my limbs.

Even though I'll baste in my own sweat, I roll up the window, blocking any ambient distractions and giving a semblance of privacy. Wiggling back into my seat—No mean feat, considering my shorts leave my thighs subject to torture by vinyl—I let Pat's sweet, melodic voice lull me into a state of semi-relaxation. Not to where I'm concentrating on the lyrics, just letting the familiar roll over my subconscious.

Eyes closed, I bring up what I'd observed of Haydn Koehler's office, focusing on the dusty, plastic palm wedged in the corner behind my intended prey, his only attempt at decorative decor. Prey is a strong word, but so is the thought that a single plastic palm and an uplight are going to make his office look chic. Besides, it sounds more impressive than looking over his shoulder.

The memory of the plant fixed in my mind, I call out to the tiny shadows cast by the uplight. Slowly, thin leaves begin to waver, tiny dust particles float freeform as they're shaken loose by the forced air from a nearby vent. I squirm in my seat, a giggle turns to a groan as my skin pulls away from the seat. My excitement over making contact nearly causes me to lose that connection. Taking a deep breath, I push past my stinging flesh and stupidity to the task at hand.

Stripes of green obscure the man seated at the desk, but at least he's in the office. I'm inside the plant, not the best vantage point. I need to push higher, the corner of the ceiling would be an ideal spot. Using my will to push and pull at the shadows, I begin jumping from one to another and then another. Through the leaves, I see movement. It's the object of my surveillance. His chair slides back and swings toward my hiding place.

"I know you're there little Schattenkind."

Shit. I pull farther into the shadowy recesses of the plant.

"Your lord and master hasn't the brains of a turnip, sending someone as untried as yourself."

Double crap. Should have known I wasn't good enough to pull this off.

"Stop skittering about in the shadows and come meet me in the flesh."

Pressure grips my shoulders and neck, sending a pounding message to my brain. Salty streams of sweat trail down my forehead, stinging my eyes and I lose what little control I have. I slam the heels of my hands against my eyes in a piss-poor attempt to shield them from the blinding brightness of the uplight. There's nothing like staring into a bare bulb—or being caught—to shake your concentration, except maybe someone tapping on your window.

Chapter 33

The double tap on my window nearly has me wetting myself. Blinking away the effects of staring into the uplight brings the person behind that tapping into view, making another set of muscles clench. As if it's not bad enough Haydn Koehler caught spying, my newest corporeal shadow, Numinous Task Force Agent Wilken, has caught me with my hand in the proverbial cookie jar.

After the NTF reassigned the disappearance of Stanley Lewis—a.k.a. The Collector—to the dark elf, I knew I'd be seeing her again. I just didn't think it would be in a parking garage in downtown Des Moines during a super-secret mission.

Rolling down the window, I try and keep a pleasant, hey-I've-got-noting-to-hide smile on my face. I kind of relish the frustration pulling at her features as she has to wait for me to roll the manual window down. No electric windows in this vintage baby.

"Hello, Miss Fey."

"Agent… I'm sorry, I've forgotten your name." I haven't, but why let her have the upper hand by admitting she's been on my mind?

Her face is as smooth and emotionless as Dara's. Wonder if there's a school bad-ass women attend to learn that trick.

"Wilken."

"Ahh, that's right. What can I do for you Agent Wilken?" Probably not the best idea to agitate an NTF agent, but what can I say? The smart ass in me can't help showing up at inappropriate times.

"Please get out of the car, Miss Fey."

She steps back, giving me room to swing the door open. I bite back a whimper of pain as my legs reluctantly lift from the seat, refusing to let her see or hear any weakness. Stalling our chat until I'm confident my voice won't be two octaves higher, I take my time closing the door. Turning, I lean against the car and cross my arms over my chest.

"So what can I do for you, Agent Wilken?"

"I know what you are."

No shit, everyone knows what I am, except me. "That makes us even, I know what you are. Nice fake tan and highlights, who's your stylist?"

Lucky for her, elves age ridiculously slow, it'll take about a million years before she develops elevens from puckering her brow. "I'm not here to talk about my hair."

"Then why are you here, Agent Wilken? Better yet, why are you following me at all?"

"What makes you think I'm following you? Feeling guilty about something?"

"So you're going to tell me it's a coincidence we're both in the same parking ramp?"

"That or fate."

Seriously? She's pulling the fate card? I can't suppress the eye roll.

"I needed a place to park, that's why I'm here. You, on the other hand, look like you were taking a nap or were you doing something more nefarious?"

"Is there a law against napping in your car?" She's really trying to get me to slip up, make a confession, something I'm so not going to do.

"Sleeping in your car in a public parking ramp in ninety-eight degree weather? I question your common sense."

I shrug. "Better than driving while I was tired."

She shakes her head. "Come on, Miss Fey, I'm not stupid. What were you doing?"

Just like everyone else, she's jumping to conclusions because of what I am. "Did you see me doing something illegal?"

"No, but—

"Then I think we're done here." I turn, grabbing the door handle, then am jerked back around. Her fingers bite into my arm as she pulls me close.

"I know what you are, I know what you've done, and Var Royd can't protect you forever."

"If you *know* what I am and what I've done, you *know* I don't need Var Royd's protection."

Her eyes widen, a grim twist to her lips as

she lets go of my arm. I could kick myself, why can't I stop and think before I open my mouth? Stepping backward, she gives me a brief nod before walking away. It's clear by my lack of thinking before speaking I do need Var Royd's protection.

Climbing back in the car, I dab the moisture gathering in the corners of my eyes. "Hel's Realm, this is no time for tears. You've got a freakin' bulldog of an NTF agent following you, get your shit together."

If I were human, I could blame it on hormones. Instead I'll chalk the tears up to insufficient sleep, frustration, and anger at my own stupidity. Twisting the rearview mirror toward me, a choked combo of laughter and sobbing slips out at the sight of my face. I'm surprised Agent Wilken was able to keep a straight face while talking to me. The full fury of Iowa's heat and humidity have taken a toll, everything is starting to melt. It's time to get out of this hotbox and out onto the open road, I may even give in and turn on the AC. My car may not have electric windows, but it does have an air conditioner. But first I really need some caffeine. Grabbing a tissue from my purse, I wipe the straying mascara from under my eyes and blot the dewy mess coating the rest of my face.

"Good enough, the barista and other coffee lovers will just have to deal with my makeup meltdown. It's not like I'm the first person to have it happen." Balling the tissue in my fist, I thrust it into my bag and toss it onto the passenger seat.

Everything in Downtown is a series of mazes, from the parking garage to avoiding going the wrong way on a one way street. By the time I reach Java Joes, my blood pressure is thumping in my ears. Somehow I manage to pull into an open space along the curb without incident, mostly because there's at least three in a row open. Gods, I hate parallel parking, damn near as much as driving in Downtown.

I get a full-frontal blast of cool air as I open the door of the coffee shop and step inside. The crunching whirl of the grinder is music to my ears and the earthy scent of beans and brew steady my shaking hands, as if the caffeine is absorbed through my skin. I'm in my own personal little slice of heaven. It's a safe place and I can relax. I don't have to think about anything except what I want in my cup. Something decadent and calorie-ridden. I deserve a treat.

Making a beeline to the counter, I scan the smatter of customers enjoying their midmorning fix and my stride falters. Oh, hel's no! At a table in the center of the room are the last two people on earth I want to see. My safe place is no longer safe. Slowly, I backup, turn tail, and slip out the door. No cup of coffee is worth the possibility of having to interact with Stasia Athory and Vana Royd.

Chapter 34

My one and only mission as Shadow is to watch Haydn Koehler and I've fucked that up royally. Not only did I not learn anything of significance, he spotted me right away. *It's time to put your Talents to work. Watch over Mr. Koehler by any means necessary.* Is it possible Var knew this would happen? Did he set me up? Or was it a ploy to get me inside Haydn's walls, using my so called female wiles to entice him into spilling his secrets? Var Royd really needs to get his godly head out of his godly ass and realize I can't hold a candle to Mata Hari, Cleopatra, or any other great femme fatale. If that's what he's looking for he should have recruited Lorelei.

Top that off with being denied my caffeinated treat because I happened to choose the same coffee shop as Stasia and Vana. What they hel are those two doing together? I guess it's not like I haven't seen them chatting before, but you wouldn't think my boss's sister would be hanging with the woman whose obsession with anti-aging   rivals her mother's. It doesn't matter that her approach is less messy—mixing blood into serums and creams instead of soaking in it—it's still stomach-churning. Then again, Vana isn't my biggest fan. Maybe they're conspiring against me. Maybe I'm overthinking again, but it's still suspicious those two were hanging out like besties. Considering they're both charter members of the Mean Girl club, it shouldn't surprise me.

Glaring at me as I toss my bag on the couch, the cat stretches and yawns.

On the way to the kitchen for some much needed fizzy caffeine, I mumble, "Sorry to disturb your majesty's midday nap."

Lucky little bastard gets to sleep whenever he wants. I'd give my right pinky toe for a nap, but that's not an option. I'm supposed to be at the Wolf Cave for my daily workout, but it's not going to happen. Not after the day I've had. Considering it's only half-way over, it can only get better. Right? The blinking red light on the answering machine screams wrong.

I pretend to ignore that nasty little light while concentrating on opening a can of Dr. Pepper without breaking a nail. Not that I can't fix it, I just don't want to waste the time and energy. Blink, blink, blink, damn red light keeps feeding the need to know the next disaster that's about to erupt, which will only be sated by pressing the button.

So I do.

The echoing, stereophonic sound of The Sisters

in prophecy mode floats from the speaker and lifts every little hair on my body to attention.

Fire holds the power of destruction. Fire holds the power of rebirth. Beware the one who wields the flame. Not all destruction is malicious. Not all rebirth is beneficial. Beware the one who wields the flame.

Thank the gods for technology like answering machines. Too bad all of their recent ramblings aren't loaded on my machine, it would make things easier, because this one is a doozy. Chilling silence fills the room as I wait for them to snap out of it and talk to me. Instead, I get a click, followed by dial tone, and the computerized voice telling me, "End of message, next message."

Miss Fey, this is Mort, I was wondering if you'd be free to talk sometime today. Again, this is Mort, please call me.

For crying out loud, how did that dim-twit get my number? Looks like the next disaster in my life can be counteracted by screening all my calls. That and watching out for the one who wields the flame, whoever the hel that is. I look down at the can of soda in my hand and contemplate adding something to it, but deep down I know it'll only make things worse.

I should try napping before work, but after The Sisters' message I've moved from tired to wired. Mort the Tweed having my home number doesn't help, either. Heading to the Wolf Cave for a vigorous workout might not be such a bad idea, then again, I'd have to deal with Teiran and Ric. So not in the mood for either of them. Calling Var and reporting on my failed mission would only add to my anxiety. Although, I could broach the subject of why his sister was meeting with Stasia Athory. Naw, not worth the hassle.

CC yawns, triggering one of my own, and we've come full circle. I might be too tired to sleep, but I can relax on the couch. A little brainless TV might help take my mind off my problems.

"Move over fur ball." I knock my bag to the floor and curl up next to the cat, flipping through the channels until I end up on one broadcasting shows from my childhood. Gotta love 70's TV. A lot was extremely controversial for the time, hel, it's controversial for the current era. Most of it couldn't be aired in this politically correct society. Screw political correctness. It's destroyed the art of conversation and learning to agree to disagree. We should be able to question everything because that's how you learn. We shouldn't have to worry about offending people who have no right to be offended. Political correctness may have started with the best of intentions, but now it's used to coddle people, push agendas, and hide the truth. Hel, my current 'assignment' is proof of that, but I'm not going to dwell on that right now.

"What do you think, CC? Ready for a little

politically incorrect TV?" I ask around a cat-inspired yawn, and sink into the softness of the cushions.

Chapter 35

So much for relaxing and a possible nap, I've wandered into Einen's realm. Or his prison, depending on how you look at it, and right now that's exactly what it feels like. The whole *like calls to like* thing is at a level ten. Not only do I sense his mood, I've taken it on myself. His anger, frustration, and fear, worst of all, the soul crushing loneliness are now mine.

The atmosphere is charged with his emotions, the oppressiveness twisting my shit mood, making me want to slit my wrists. The lawn and gardens are dead or dying, thick with the stench of rotten vegetation. The sky is dark and dreary, ominous clouds continuously rolling overhead. The house feels like the afterparty of a funeral. Shadows gather in every space, and their high-pitched keening makes my eardrums throb and skin prickle with gooseflesh. It's a gods awful sound, far worse than the cries of remorse by any other species.

"I miss him too, but it's not like he's dead."

My words seem to shake them out of their grief and they flock around me, their mood lifting. I pick up bits and pieces of their jumbled chatter, more feeling and scraps of mental images than actual words. They can't reach him. There are only two ways I can think of to cut Einen off from shadow: absolute darkness or absolute light. Teiran once made my bedroom so dark it chased the shadows away and Var used light to banish them from the salon. There's always the possibility there's another way, I just don't know what it would be, any more than I know what the key to his room looks like, or where Vana has hidden it. If I could find it, we'd all be happier.

"I don't suppose any of you saw what Vana used to lock the door?" It's a longshot, but what the hel? It's not like I have anyone else to ask. The only thing Einen told me was who locked him in, not how it was done.

Maybe this was a bad idea since coherent communication isn't high on the list of a shadow's skill set. Trying to decipher their jumble of sights, sounds, and smells has me on my knees, clutching my head. The wall holding back my Talents wavers and fails. I scream as it falls and a flood of flickering, distorted pictures pushes through my head. Dark patches form in my peripheral vision, slowly taking over my sight. Walls, ceiling, and floor begin to spin. My stomach heaves and I gag, choking on my last meal, a half-drained can of soda. Pain becomes synonymous with breathing and my ears ring with the bizarre language of shadows.

They know I'm hurting and it scares them, but their fear intensifies the torture inflicted on my mind and body as I involuntarily take it on. With the protective wall gone, anything dead or dying calls out to me, ripping loose another scream.

I need to get out, get back to my body, back to my apartment. If I stay here, I have no doubt I'll either go crazy or die fighting for my sanity. Too bad I don't have a pair of ruby slippers to click while I chant, "There's no place like home."

Pushing away my surroundings, the shadows, and the dead things crying out to me, I call up pictures of home. Memories of my furnishings, my rooms, and my cat. Call me crazy, but I can hear CC screeching.

His cries are faint at first, but gradually gain volume over the ruckus around me until he dominates the noise in my head. That touchstone with reality gives me the strength to shove the sensory overload into a box and slam the lid. Shadows recede, their chattering softened to whispers. The wall, maybe not with ease, but back where it belongs. The dead are once again silent.

"Thank you," I whisper, loosening my hold on the connection between myself and CC. This isn't the first time my furry buddy saved my ass. He came to my rescue once when The Collector invaded my personal space, and a few times when I was so deep in a dream I couldn't get out by myself. He damn sure deserves a special treat when I get home.

Confidence restored, I look to the contrite shadows circling me and contemplate standing. Between the way my muscles jitter and jump along with the floaty feeling in my head, it's probably better I stay where I am. "Let's try this again, can any of you tell me about the key to Einen's room?"

I hold up a hand as the chattering raises in pitch and volume. "One at a time, please, or better yet, pick a spokesman." There's no way in hel, I can deal with all of them trying to tell me at once.

Some of the smaller, ghostly shapes move toward the back of the group, leaving a handful huddled together, conversing. They must be stronger. They're not as faded in color or opacity, but more solid in form, in deeper, richer shades of black and grey. They have none of the ragged, wispy edges, or paler shades of grey and smoke like the others. I wonder if they are older, and because of that, more powerful.

The group breaks and steps back, revealing a single form. My jaw drops as it steps toward me. Could it be? Is it possible? Looking at this shadow reminds me how much I have to learn. It's as close to fully formed as a shadow can be, not just a shape with undistinguishable features. It may not be perfect and sharply detailed, but that form is undeniably Einen. I wonder if the two are connected on a deeper level. Is this shadow Einen's true shadow, or one that mimics its master?

I climb to my feet, stepping toward it, my curiosity overriding my common sense. My hand passes through thick, substantial air instead of landing on his cheek. His opaque appearance is deceiving. I don't know what I expected, he's still a shadow. Thin, imperfectly shaped lips curl upward and if those dark pits were eyes, I imagine they would be filled with laughter.

He mimics my action, his hand rests against my cheek, It's cool and slightly firm. Almost like the real thing, yet empty. There's none of the spark that ignites between Einen and I when we touch. All it manages to do is remind me of the void in my soul that Einen fills. And the intense desire to find that damn key so I can touch the real thing.

"So tell me, Shadow Copy, do you know what the key is?"

A familiar smirk and tilt of the head brings a smile to my face, obviously he finds the name amusing and best of all, he knows something.

Chapter 36

"Gods, woman, when was the last time you slept?" Lorelei's brilliant blue eyes stare at me in the mirror. With soup-can-sized rollers covering her head, it would be comical if I wasn't dragging ass so early in the evening.

Every girl wants to hear they look like crap. "I'll remember to put more concealer under my eyes next time."

She twirls the chair to face me. "Hardy har har. Seriously, what's going on?"

"I've been busy."

"Too busy to sleep?"

I shrug. Not really wanting to go into detail, I fudge a little. "I squeeze it in when I can, sometimes it's just hard to get there."

Her brow raises and I feel like a child about to be scolded. "Usually, busy people have no problem getting there."

"You can't tell me you've never had a time when you couldn't sleep."

A slow smile creeps across her face. "I usually find something to wear me out, then I sleep like a baby."

"You mean *someone*, don't you?"

She shrugs. "It's not like you don't know a few good looking specimens who could wear you out. Like, oh, I don't know, a couple of pretty âlfar?"

"Now you sound like Nyssa. Speaking of, she's got the dryer ready for you. Off you go."

Her laughter weaves a trail of warmth behind her and I shake my head. If it were only that easy to find what Rey affectionately terms, a fuck buddy. As pretty as my elves are, they aren't fuck buddy material, and to suggest an arrangement like that would only cause problems, which is the last thing the three of us need. It's bad enough I'm attracted to both of them. Besides, sex is not the answer to my sleeping issues.

My waking life needs to change. Who has time for sex, let alone sleep, with the list of crap I'm juggling? A second job I never asked for, finding a key that's not a key, self-defense and Talent training, and more, all on top of my regular job. Erasing my debt to the goddess of death would make sleeping a lot easier when I do create time.

"You okay, Keely?"

"Fine. Why?"

Nyssa frowns at me, the tiny hamster turning the wheel in her head running at double speed. "You shivered."

"May have to back the AC down, it's a little chilly in here."

"You sure that's it? Lorelei and I were just talking about how tired you look."

"Didn't get much sleep today, no biggy."

"How come?"

I roll my eyes, body falling into an indignant, boneless stance reminiscent of my teen years. "What's with everyone being so concerned about my sleep?"

"Because we're your friends and we worry about you. Besides, Dara will have a cow if she has to pick up the slack when you decide to fall over during your shift."

The last statement and her mischievous grin pull the sting from my reply. "I highly doubt we'll have any calves running around the cutting floor tonight. Besides, there's always Rey."

Rey sticks his tongue out at me and I blow him a kiss as we head toward the break room.

"If you say so, but it would keep the night interesting, considering all the blue-hair gossip is way too boring," Nyssa says. "I don't know about you, but I don't need to hear about the latest grocery store escapades."

Maybe I'm too tired to understand. "Huh? The little old ladies are having grocery store escapades?"

She sighs in disappointment. "It's not what you think, trust me."

"I take it you found out sexcapades and escapades are two different things?"

Her bottom lip protrudes. "I also found out thumping melons means exactly that, thumping melons."

"Poor Nyssa, I'm sure someone will come in with something juicy."

"Whatever. Win asked me to find out if you have time for a walk-in. What do you want me to tell her?"

"Male or female?"

"Male." She tries to keep a straight face, but the gleam in her eyes screams, *I know something you don't know.*

"Just a cut?"

She nods.

"A regular?"

She shakes her head.

"Do I know him?"

She shrugs.

"Fine, whatever." Any other time I'd be happy to play games with her, but I'm not feeling it tonight. "Tell Win to give me a minute or two then send him back"

With a grin, she gracefully exits to reception on what are probably four inch heels. Gravity is definitely that little nixie's friend. I'd fall over wearing them, especially if I had her upper body endowments. If I had her curves, finding a bed buddy would probably be easier.

Get your mind out of the gutter, Keely. I blame

Lorelei and Nyssa for putting the idea in my head. In truth, my mind is being tugged in too many directions to concentrate on sex or work right now. I want time to sit and research the terms Mort gave me and I want to go back to Einen's to chat with his shadow doppelgänger. When it came down to it, communicating with him wasn't easy, but it was informative. I think I could learn a ton from him, and it's tempting to leave Einen where he is and team up with Shadow Copy, now affectionately known as SC.

Taking a deep breath, I follow her back to the cutting room and force myself to set up my station for the mystery client. At least, I know it's a he and just a cut. Easy peasy, right?

My jaw drops when he rounds the corner, and the first instinct is to get the hel out of Dodge. Run fast, hop in the car, and drive even faster. Leave the state if I have to. Hel, leave the country. Anything to get out of the situation I'm standing in front of.

Haydn Koehler smiles and holds out his hand. "I thought we should meet in the flesh, Miss Fey, or should I use your title? The Lord's Shadow."

Chapter 37

The usual dull roar of conversation stopped the minute he rounded the corner. My shoulders bunch with the weight of a million eyes on me and my mouth and brain struggle to connect. It doesn't help that he's sexy as hel, there's just something about a man in a dress shirt and jeans.

"Mr. Koehler." It's pointless to pretend I don't know who he is. Grabbing my cape, I turn the chair toward him. "Have a seat."

Watching the big man fold himself into my chair is a sight to behold. He's as graceful as my elven counterparts, with more than a touch of primal. Not animalistic, like Teiran and his hound form, something… I don't know, just… Otherworldly.

Yes, there's an otherworldliness to all Enchants, but this is different. I can't put my finger on it, just like I couldn't figure out what Var was when I met him. Maybe that's the ticket, he's something more than an En. Something substantial, something old. No, old isn't the right term. Var, Vana, and Hel feel old, but gods should, they've been around the block a few more times than we have. Haydn

Koehler feels older, like he's been here since the beginning of time. Ancient. Yeah, he feels ancient.

I whirl the cape around him, letting it rest across his massiveness while I adjust his collar. Collared shirts need to be tucked into themselves to keep the hair clippings from gathering inside. There is nothing worse than bits of hair embedded into the fabric and coming back to haunt you later. That's why stylists spend a quarter of their time shopping. There comes a time when you have to toss your work clothes in the trash. I've taken to burning mine when I dispose of the salon's clippings using witchfire. Witchfire burns cold and leaves nothing behind, not even ash. Since The Collector debacle, I've been über careful about the disposal of hair. The last thing I want to hear about is someone else using clippings to control Ens.

"And how would you like your hair cut, Mr. Koehler?" I ask, fighting with the closure of the cape. The smirk on his face makes me want to force it closed, but I'm not that rude. Finally giving up, I use a clip to hold it in place. The man's neck is just too broad for a standard cape and I don't own a larger one.

"A trim, please. I like it a little on the shaggy side."

"So clean up your neck and sideburns?"

He shrugs. "If that's what you think it needs."

Running my hands through the rich red locks,

I assess his current style and the movement and growth patterns of the hair. Like Ric's blond, Haydn's red holds every shade possible. There's also a nice amount of body, not curly or uncontrollable, just nice waves. The kind that lend themselves to easy styling.

"Clean up the perimeter, a little texturizing and shaping."

"You're the expert, my style—or lack of—is in your hands."

The corner of my mouth tugs upward when he winks. On the charm meter he's hitting an eight or nine. I wave Nyssa over. "This is Nyssa, our shampoo girl, Mr. Koehler. If you'll follow her over to the shampoo bowl, she'll get you prepped for me."

His eyebrows nearly touch his hairline. "I'm to be denied one of Keely's famous shampoos?"

"Huh?" I'm a little more than confused, where would he get a line like that?

He gives Nyssa a panty wetting smile. "No offense, you beautiful creature."

Head dipped, falsies fluttering, she giggles. "None taken, you big hunk of burning love."

What the—

Nyssa slaps her hand over her mouth, spins on her heels, and practically runs toward the break room.

Wow. What the hel just happened? It was as

if a switch had been flipped on and then off again. It takes a lot to embarrass Nyssa, but this guy succeeded with her own words. Her work filter was not only down, but nonexistent. I'm going to have to pay special attention to my words before they're allowed to leave my mouth. Then again, after what I witnessed, I may not have a choice.

Turning the chair, I wave toward the shampoo bowls. "Let's get you shampooed."

He unfolds himself from the chair as gracefully as he entered it, and I have a hard time not enjoying the view of tight muscles under their denim skin.

I pull the chair out and have him scooch down as far as possible as I lean it back. Once he's in position, I grab the hose and turn on the water. "Hope that isn't too uncomfortable, Mr. Koehler. Like the cape, these things aren't built for the big and tall."

He smiles up at me as I run the water over his head. "I'm quite comfortable, and call me Haydn. You don't mind if I call you Keely, do you?"

I shake my head. "It's what most people call me."

It's not the same effect he had on Nyssa, but I find myself drawn in by his charm. His demeanor is so different from what I expected, not that I really know what I expected. With as big as he is, tough guy comes to mind. With his profession, I'd assume assertive to the point of being pushy. So far he's neither.

"Forgive me for asking for personal treatment, but I wanted to get you away from prying ears."

If lack of prying ears is what he wants, then he picked the perfect time to show up since Dara won't be in until sundown. Rey can probably hear him, but I doubt he's listening. One, he's swamped with his usual flock of blue-hairs. Two, he knows better than to eavesdrop on me. As he puts it, 'here if you need me, but don't want to get pulled into the drama.' For once, he's the smart one of the group.

"Okay," I say, massaging the shampoo into Haydn's hair and scalp.

"Mmm, that feels good. No wonder Grace said to make sure I have you shampoo me."

I'd forgotten all about the interview I'd done for the Iowa Star, it feels like a million years ago, instead of a few months. Rinsing away the suds, I contemplate asking what he wants to say that needs privacy.

My stomach flutters and lady parts tingle when he moans. If my scalp manipulations are pleasurable enough to illicit a moan like that, imagine what it would be like if we were doing something else.

I glance around the room and yep, everyone is staring. Heat rises in my cheeks. I yank my hands away from his head and grab the hose.

"Done so soon?" His tiger-eye irises are

almost non-existent behind the enlarged pupils.

Maybe I should switch to cold and use it for more than rinsing his hair. Grabbing a towel, I drape it over his head and help him sit up.

"Tell me, Keely, would you have dinner with me tomorrow night?"

Chapter 38

There's a vampire on a red Valkyrie, clothed in Nazi regalia, and a blood-drenched woman possessively clinging to him. A hound howls, pulling at the oversized chain around his neck held by the half-dead, half-living goddess of Helheim. Mist writhes across the ground like hands grasping at straws. It begins to solidify. Take form. That form is the thing of nightmares. My nightmares. Stanley Lewis, aka The Collector. His arm raises, finger pointing, his mouth moving in silent words. The mist swirling around his legs climbs, engulfs him, then lowers to reveal a real-world nightmare. Agent Wilken stands in his place, pointing at me.

Laying in bed, gasping for breath and sweating like a marathon runner, I stare at the ceiling. Stanley Lewis is the thing of my nightmares, not only because of his actions, but my own. I killed him. Him dissolving into Agent Wilken only solidifies that nightmare. Crushed between the mattress and my guilt, I fight back tears. The desire to get out of bed and start my day is nonexistent. All I want to do is lay here in my own headspace and wallow. Ric said guilt will keep me from becoming the monster The Collector was. He also said it would become easier to deal with in time. I wonder how much time is enough.

Sniffling, I roll onto my side, using the corner of the sheet to wipe my eyes. The clock reads eleven. I'm up early, way too early. It's just one of the many ways bad dreams fuck you over. Another is keeping you from falling back to sleep. As much as I'd like to lay here and feel sorry for myself, it can't happen. I have to put on my big girl panties, take a shower, and make some coffee, not necessarily in that order. My dance card is full with an afternoon of getting my ass kicked in the name of training and a date with the fiery Haydn Koehler, neither of which can be ignored. Have I said how much I hate my new job?

Getting up, I strip the bed, tossing the bundle of sweat and tear laden sheets in the corner. I'll do the laundry when I get to it, not like it's a high priority. Probably a level four or five. Coffee on the other hand, that's level one, urgent.

Cold-brewed latte in hand, I divert to my pseudo office, sucking caffeine down while the prehistoric computer boots. Logging in takes long enough to finish and refill my glass, but at least I don't have dialup. I'd have a hel of a caffeine buzz using my refill timing method.

I'd never noticed the sparseness of the room before Teiran moved in with me, not that he brought a ton of personal items. Hel, he was my roomie for only a few weeks, but the room feels empty without the arrogant jerk. Not that I'll ever admit it to him, or anyone else for that matter. And I certainly don't want him moving back, no matter how much I miss his organizational and cleaning skills, waking to the scent of fresh brewed coffee, or the gourmet meals. Despite those perks, I enjoy having my privacy and alone time back. There's no way I'd be sitting here searching the internet for terms I can barely pronounce, let alone spell, if he were here. If he saw what I was doing he'd go all big bad wolf on me.

I have no idea why he's so opposed to me finding out what I'm capable of, especially when it's his boss who wants me to learn. Hel, everyone is opposed to it and it all comes back to whatever Einen did in the past. They need to get over it and realize I'm not Vereinen and it's better I know. That way, there's less chance of me accidentally repeating history.

Thank the gods for Google and its ability to guess what I'm trying to find. It's not like I'm a terrible speller, but I need all the help I can get finding words I didn't know existed. Necrokinesis isn't on your average high school spelling list, at least not the high school I attended. And it sure wasn't on the curriculum at beauty school. Hel, I doubt there are college courses that touch on this subject, but I could be wrong. Actually, it's not a bad idea and wouldn't kill me to look into it. Finding time might hurt a bit, but it wouldn't kill me.

There's an amazing amount of stuff on necrokinesis centering on gaming, but very little on real world application. More digging in gaming terms turns up shadowkinesis, that's a word I can get into. It's defined as the manipulation of shadows, which sounds about right. I hit the print icon, there's no way I'll remember this stuff if I don't make a copy. Yeah, I could bookmark the page, but there's no guarantee my flaky computer won't crash and burn. A little further down the list is umbrakinesis, the manipulation of darkness. That would be more along the lines of Teiran's Talents. There has to be some kernel of truth in this crap, they didn't make it up out of thin air, since everything is based on something. The whole myth-and-make-believe-verses-fact discussion was quashed in the 80's when Enchants stepped into the spotlight.

It could be that I'm looking at this all wrong. I'm not a real girl, I'm a character in a video game. Wouldn't that be convenient? I could just sit here and wait for some inept player to kill me off. Wouldn't it be awesome to have even less control over my life than I do?

Wyrd and ørlög. Fate and destiny. Could be

everyone is right. No matter what path I take, it's inevitable that I'll end up with the same fate? Driven batshit by the power? Locked in a room for eternity after attempting to take over the world? It's the curse of the Schattenkind—lose yourself in the power and eventually go mad.

Sulking, I roll the chair away from the desk. Sure, the power is intoxicating, but it doesn't control me. I need to figure out how to control it. It belongs to me, not the other way around.

"Damn it, I refuse to be what they expect."

Chapter 39

Teiran tightens his hold on my wrist, his thumb pressing between the bones, and my fingers loosen their grip on the shears trapped between us. "You stink."

Backed against the wall there's nowhere for me to go but down. Letting my body go limp, I slide down the wall and dangle from his grasp. With a bit of wiggling, I manage to connect my elbow with the side of his kneecap. Stars flash before my eyes and a whimper escapes. Why the hel is it called a funny bone? It's not funny at all. He grunts, his body jerks sideways, and he steps back to regain his balance, leaving me the opening I'd been looking for. My fist connects with his man bits. He doubles over in pain and releases my wrist.

I half crawl, half slither across the floor until I'm out of reach. What I'd done was pretty lowbrow on the fighting spectrum, but all's fair in love and war. And it's almost always war with Teiran, even when he's in a *loving* mood. "So do you. It happens when it's ninety in the shade and during work outs."

If looks could kill, I'd be dead and I don't think it's entirely due to the crotch shot. Even Ric looks taken aback by my actions. Not that I expected him to give me a standing O for using a low blow to get out of the situation.

"The stench I speak of has nothing to do with the heat, or working out."

"And what pray tell, do you credit this *stench* with?" I ask, climbing to my feet with the help of Ric's outstretched hand.

Finally standing straight, but still feeling the effects, Teiran continues to murder me with his gaze. "Shadow and sulfur."

Shadow I can understand, but sulfur? What the hel would make me smell like sulfur? It's not like I've been hanging out in the bowels of a volcano, or the hel with two l's. I'm not even sure if it's real. Then again, why not? Elves, vampires, and helhounds are real, and gods walk the earth.

"I have no idea why I'd smell like sulfur, but shadow is part of my DNA, deal with it."

"I believe what Teiran is trying to say, is that the shadow he smells is… not of your usual chemistry."

Great, just great, I stink like Einen. Good to know that no matter what kind of scented body wash I use, I'll always carry back a souvenir from my visits. One that will alert everyone to where I've been, proven by this exchange and Var claiming to smell it on me after the last time I visited Vereinen. Yanking my hand from Ric's warm grasp, I roll my eyes. "Could it be because I've been using my

Talents as ordered by your lord and master?"

"Our lord and master," Teiran reminds me. Like I need reminding of the giant hemorrhoid that's attached himself to me.

"I suppose it would be possible, but still, you do smell different, yet familiar."

I jerk away as Ric leans in and sniffs my hair. He tries to hide the rejection of my movement and a part of me almost feels bad, but he invaded my personal space. And I'm sorry, sniffing me is creepy, especially from a vamp. Not that it would be any different if Teiran were to lean in and get a snort-full. I can't think of a single situation where a predator sniffing you doesn't lead to the possibility of bad things happening. So sue me for not wanting to test that theory.

"What about the sulfur? Is it my body wash? Or shampoo? How about the chemicals I use at work?" I know I'm grasping at straws, but there has to be a logical explanation, and it diverts the conversation away from my visiting Einen.

"I would suspect you have come in contact with an En who can wield fire. Do any of your clients have that ability?"

I shake my head. That would easily explain it all away, but I seriously don't know. It's not like I keep a record of what Talents my clients do or don't have. Maybe I should start, especially if there are going to be pop quizzes in the future.

"She could have picked up the scent anywhere." Teiran moves to Ric's side, his homicidal gaze reduced to injure, with a side of disable. "Have you been anywhere other than your residence or place of business?"

"Yeah." The childish streak in me has me one wording it, and shaking or nodding my head. Sure, I want to know the answer, but something about irritating Teiran makes my day a little brighter. And today, I need all the brightening I can get.

"It would help if you could elaborate, Keely."

Irritating Ric doesn't push my buttons the same way and I'm feeling a tad bit bad about him being collateral damage in this war of wills. Softening my resolve to stick to one word sentences and head movements, I try for a real sentence. "I went Downtown to do some recon for my big spy mission."

"Your mission?" Ric's features twist a bit, then smooth out. "I think we have found the origin of the sulfur scent."

Chapter 40

At least Haydn agreed to do this date thing on my turf. I'm within walking distance of my home, surrounded by people I know. Not that most of them would lift a finger to help me, or even call the cops. Hel, the cops wouldn't help me if the crime was committed right in front of them. They still think I conspired with The Collector and would love to see me go down. Well, they'll have to get in line and it's a long one.

I have a love/hate relationship with asking questions and the answers I receive. I love knowing, but I hate knowing what I'm walking into. Scratch that, I hate not knowing *enough* about what I'm walking into.

The sulfur smell quite possibly came from Haydn Koehler, that's all my idiot partners would tell me. You'd think they'd want me better prepared, but all I got was "need to know" bullshit from Teiran, and "you'll be fine" from Ric. They didn't even offer to tail me. I know, it's my job, but the offer of backup would have been nice. Not that I want them to, it could make things worse on several levels. Like, I don't know, piss my 'date' off, or keep him from trusting and confiding in me. And I need that trust or I'm screwed six ways to Sunday with Var. He's been patient up till now—as patient as his controlling personality will allow—but I don't know how much longer that will last.

Entering Basement Brews, I'm kicking myself for not waiting till sundown. Dara would have jumped at the chance to watch my back. Then again, I hadn't even told her about my date, let alone the assignment to infiltrate Haydn's inner circle. Hel's Realm, she is going to be so pissed that I kept something from her again, but she keeps shit from me all the time. Guess we're even, not that she'll see it that way.

"One?" asks the hostess with a dutiful smile. Is she covering up her nervousness at seating a schattenkind? Does she think I'm going to let my shadows feast on her?

"No, I'm meeting someone."

Her smile broadens. Maybe I'm reading too much into people's reactions, that might have been a pity smile. Why would she pity me for eating alone? It's not like I *can't* get a date. I rethink that letting my shadows feast on her bit.

Damn it, Keely, stop over-thinking things.

"Want to take a look and see if your party is here?"

"Yeah, thanks." I step around her and search the room. Even way off in the corner, his red hair and size stand out, making him an easy target. Let's hope he's an easy target in other ways, because master spy, I am not. "I see him, he's over there."

Her mouth drops as she eyeballs the behemoth that is my date. "Oh, you're meeting Mr. Koehler. Why didn't you say so?"

I shrug, walking past her and her questioning expression. Gossip makes the world go around, especially in The Meadows, and I'm not about to add to it by opening my mouth.

"Hello, Keely," he says, standing. "I'm so glad you could make it, you look lovely." His gaze runs from the top of my head to the floor, lingering on certain aspects that negate the gentlemanly act of pulling out my chair.

Not that I'm complaining, or haven't done the same to the opposite sex. The lingering once-over, not the pulling out a chair. I've contemplated pulling Teiran's chair out from under him, but that's nowhere near the same thing.

"Thanks, I was worried my makeup would melt, or my hair would frizz on the way over here."

His laughter is as big and attention grabbing as his size, and every eye in the place is on us. So much for keeping a low profile, like it was going to happen anyway. Everyone knows who we are and they're all going to be speculating what we're doing together. It bears repeating, gossip makes the world go around.

"I do love a woman with a sense of humor. Do you know what you'd like to drink?"

Smiling, I nod. "Of course."

He waves his hand and seemingly out of thin air, the waitress appears. "The lady is ready to order."

I usually start with a something light, end with something dark. Feeling the need to shake it up, I combine the two. "A black and tan, please."

"Make that two."

The girl nods and hurries off to the bar. My discomfort with being alone with him, leaves me hoping she hurries back just as fast. It's kind of funny how all my recent 'dates' revolve around drinking. Coffee with Ric. Wine with Var. Beer with Ric. Coffee with Ric and Teiran. Beer with Haydn. Well, not all of those were dates and some did involve food. Where was I going with this? Damn, at least I'm not rambling out loud. Gotta kick Nervous Nelly out of the driver's seat. Where is that girl with my beer?

"Keely? Earth to Keely."

"What?" Damn, have to get out of my own head and pay attention. "Sorry."

"You were pretty deep in thought. Mind if I ask what you where thinking about?"

"Sorry, it was nothing, just scheduling conflicts I need to take care of at work."

"It must be difficult pleasing everyone."

Okay, then, small talk it is, but I have a feeling he's setting the groundwork for something much bigger. After all he is a reporter at heart. Put the subject at ease and slowly squeeze the information out without them noticing.

"There are occasions when you have to disappoint someone." Where the hel is my beer?

He opens his mouth, but closes it as our drinks appear.

"Are you ready to order dinner or do you need a few more minutes?" asks the waitress.

"Are you ready, Keely?"

I hadn't even glanced at the menu. Then again, besides the nightly specials I have it memorized. "Sure, go ahead."

"How do you feel about pizza?"

"I don't hate it."

"Sausage, mushroom, and onion?"

I nod. "Sounds great." How the hel did he know what my favorite toppings are?

"What size?" asks our waitress, jotting down the order.

"Is large okay with you?"

"That depends on how hungry you are."

He grins at me. "Are you insinuating I eat a lot?"

"Well, you're not a small guy." I turn to the waitress. "Better make it an extra-large."

"My thoughts exactly," she says with a grin

and a wink, before rushing off to turn in the order.

"Now that that's out of the way, maybe you'd like to discuss why you were playing with the shadows in my office."

And just like that, the art of subtlety disappears, taking my ability to make words along for the ride.

"Come on, Keely, you know I saw you. I just want to know why you were there."

My mouth opens and then closes, I got nothing. Or should I say, nothing that's not going to get me in deep do-do with someone, doesn't matter who.

Sighing, he shakes his head. "Don't pretend I left you speechless, you had to have an inkling I'd bring this up."

"Yeah, kinda figured you would."

"So just tell me what the hel Var Royd wants."

"What makes you think it was Var's idea?"

He leans back in his chair, eyes narrowed, lips pursed. "You seriously want me to believe, Var didn't put you up to it?"

I do the only thing I can do, the safest thing, sit there and keep my mouth shut.

"Whatever he's got on you, must be pretty good to keep you this tight lipped. You do know you don't have to be afraid of him."

I open my mouth—

"Don't bother saying you're not afraid of him or that he's not forcing you to do his dirty work. I know him better than that."

"Fine, he wants you to stop trashing him in the media."

There it is again, that big booming laughter and it doesn't stop until the pizza is on the table. A response I never expected.

Chapter 41

"He thinks by sending you, I'll stop talking about what a dick he is? Excuse my French, what a jerk he is?" He lifts a slice of pizza onto my plate.

I shrug. "Excused, and what can I say, he seems to think I'm intimidating."

"I suppose you are, but not in the way he thinks."

I fight the urge to squirm in my chair. I've seen his powers of flirtation, but having them focused on you makes a difference. You get the feeling he means every word he says, no matter how ungrounded in reality.

Between bites Haydn chuckles.

I grin. "Keep that up and you're going to choke." This isn't exactly how I expected this conversation to go, nor did I intend on liking him. Haydn Koehler was supposed to be my mark, nothing more. It's possible that bonding over pizza, beer, and a mutual distaste of Var Royd—although I'll never say it out loud—helps.

"I can't help it, he hasn't changed in all the years I've known him. Arrogant little bastard, again excuse my French."

"Don't worry about it, your French doesn't offend me at all. Matter of fact, I'm fairly fluent myself. You've known Var a long time?"

His laughter is contagious, so full of joy and life. There is a twelve year old boy lurking just beneath the surface and it makes him all the more likable. "You got it, no more apologies and yes. He and I go way back. We've never been what you would call friends, but over the years he's become more and more full of himself. He needs to be taken down a peg."

"And you're the guy to do it?"

"So they say, but I don't intend on taking him down quite the way they intended."

"Who's they? The other Var Royd haters in the world?"

He shrugs, licking pizza sauce from his fingers. "You know what he is, the things he's done and yet, you joined his little… crew."

Conversation over, time to get back to what he came for. "I had no choice."

"Keely, my dear, we always have choices."

"Okay, fine, my choice was the lesser of several evils."

His brows shoot skyward. "Really? You find everything Ingvar has done to be an evil of a lesser extent than anything else you faced?"

I shrug, not knowing how to answer, especially since I don't know *everything* he's ever done. Would it have been so evil to give Stasia a little blood in exchange for some extra cash? I could have negotiated enough to get myself out of debt. And the NTF? They're not evil, they're just doing their job. I know what I did was wrong, evil if you will, but I don't want to spend the rest of my life in the Enchant Containment Unit. One stint in the C.U. was enough. What about Hel? Ultimately, I'm working for her. She's the one who wanted me to take the position of Shadow. She may have influenced everything around me to leave me no reasonable choice. Are any of these things less evil than Var?

And who's to say what's evil or good? Hel herself chastised me for putting things in black and white terms. How'd she put it? Something about, 'there's no black or white, just shades between.' Considering what I'd done and how I use Var as a shield against further punishment, am I any less evil than what I've faced?

Maybe I should have run away. That might have solved some of my problems, but not all of them. Var Royd would have found me no matter where I ran and his anger would have washed over anyone who helped me. Hel's wrath would have rivaled his and, with her power over the dead, I will never escape her hold. In the end, what's done is done.

"I made my choice, now I have to live with

it. There's no turning back. Besides, I seem to have been pushed toward this ending, who am I to fight fate?"

"We all have choices, Keely. Ørlög and wyrd are built on those choices. The nornir may weave our life span and have the ability to cut it short, but we make the choices that get us from point A to point B. If it were true that some great force controlled our destiny, our end game, things that were long ago prophesied would have already come to pass."

"What the hel's that supposed to mean?"

"It means you're not stuck being Royd's lackey. What if I could offer you a way out?"

"Okay, stop right there, I'm tired of people making me offers they can't uphold, or better yet, offers I can't refuse."

He tosses his head back, deep, rich laughter radiates waves of warmth in the space around him. The suspicions are now fact. His Talent involves fire, it's the only explanation behind the heat that emanates off of him. Not to mention the flame inspired shades of his hair and eyes.

Beware the one who wields the flame.

I'd always thought Annya's hair and eyes reminded me of flames and fire, but Hayden Koehler has her beat by a long shot. Annya is the warmth of home and hearth, Hayden is a raging inferno.

Beware the one who wields the flame.

When his Talents surface, he's stunning. With them dampened, his features are only slightly above average. Unless you're into rugged masculinity, topped with boyish charm. In truth, not a bad combo, but the last thing I need is to let him or his charm distract me.

Beware the one who wields the flame.

"I tell you what. You pretend to infiltrate my 'organization' to appease his lordship and I'll let you follow me around."

"What do you get out of this?"

"Why the best thing possible, a piece of lovely arm candy to show off at gatherings and events."

"Let me guess, you want me to play double agent."

He shrugs. "If you happened to tell me what Var is up to I can't stop you."

The twelve year old boy is back with a playful wink and lopsided grin. The corners of my own mouth refuse to stay down or even neutral, although The Sister's words continue to bang at my brain.

Beware the one who wields the flame.

Chapter 42

I'm feeling pretty damn good after my meeting with Haydn. Too good. It shouldn't have been this easy to get into his inner circle. Yeah, I know I'm never going to be truly one of the insiders and he not so subtly hinted I should keep him in the loop on all things Var Royd. That was kind of to be expected, but there's still something hinky about the whole thing. Why was he so into bring me into his fold? Is he another power player who wants to use me?

Hel's Realm, I'm not feeling so great anymore.

The spicy-sweet scent of clove greets me as I open the door. In the dim light, cast by the tiny luminaries on the steps, sits the accompanying female form.

"Hey, Dara." I pull the door shut behind me and flip the locks, both manmade and magical.

"You are quite the social butterfly. Dinner with Haydn Koehler? How did you meet him?"

I take a seat on the step slightly below her and sigh. "It wasn't a date, not in the true sense. He's been running a smear campaign against Var."

"Let me guess, the Sun King wants you to

take care of him." She taps the cigarette against the ashtray at her side.

"When you put it like that it sounds all mobster." I grin at her, but she isn't reciprocating. "My orders were to spy on him, that's all."

"In my book, spying does not mean you have to date him. With your Talents you should be able to do this spying from afar."

"True, but he caught me and that's what led to the *date*."

I have the ability to see better than the average bear in dim light because of my Talents. Not that I need to see the aggravation she displays. From the eye roll and shaking head, to the sigh and slap of her hand on her thigh, it's so un-Dara-esque it's shockingly apparent in every way.

"How did you get caught? What the fuck was the Sun King thinking? Why would he send you in untested? Why would Koehler let this indiscretion pass with a simple dinner date? What did he truly want?"

"Slow down, one question at a time."

Taking a drag off her cigarette, she blows the perfumed stream upward. "Fine, how did you get caught?"

"I attempted to use the shadows in his plastic palm to watch and listen in. He must have sensed me, when he turned to look I panicked and lost control. Agent Wilken tapping on my window didn't help."

"What? You did not mention Wilken, and how was she able to tap on your window? Does she have the Talent of levitation?"

"Guess I should have clarified, I was in my car in the parking ramp."

Another drag and forceful blow.

"I tried reaching his offices from the apartment, but it didn't work. I needed to see his offices in person, so I joined a student tour group."

She opens her mouth and I hold up a hand to stop her from asking more questions. "Don't worry, I used a disguise. I was in my car because I thought it would be easier to be in proximity of my target. Which it was, but that left me open to invasion by snooping NTF agents—

"Where the hel were your partners? They should have been there to watch your back."

"I have no idea where they were, I didn't tell them I was going."

"I say this in the nicest, most well meaning way possible." Her clenched jaw and steely eyes belay this statement. "What the fuck were you thinking?"

I know she's mad, but the flying f-bombs scare the bejesus out of me. Rey is the flinger of bombs, not Dara.

"I thought I could handle it on my own." As soon as it's out of my mouth, I know it was the wrong thing to say.

"You most certainly cannot handle this on your

own. Just because you carry those shears at your side and have the Talent to do the job, doesn't mean you are ready, in any way, shape, or form. I was against you getting messed up with Var Royd from the beginning and this only cements that desire. You have no idea the magnitude of the battle he has placed you in the center of."

"Then why don't you enlighten me?"

Slouched, elbows on knees, she cradles her head in her hands. "I cannot."

"Can't or won't?"

"Can. Not."

Her building anger is rubbing off on me, kicking my sarcasm gene into overdrive. "Let me guess, it's a vamp thing, or maybe it's your damn goddess's orders."

She palms the cigarette, snuffing it out and tosses it to the side. Even with the lack of light, I see her pupils contract into thin, catlike slits. Every sense screams stop, but it's too late to close the floodgates.

"You say you have my back. You say we're friends. What the fuck, Dara?" I'm on my feet now, getting in her personal space. "I thought we worked past the bullshit, but if you're going to keep waffling how am I supposed to trust—

She's toe to toe with me, her sheer presence backing me down the stairs. "Do not even speak to me of trust, you have hid—

"Maybe you're in the need to know categ—

"And to protect you, I need to know ev—

"Screw that, you know I can't tell you every… thing." All my anger and energy are washed away as my words hit me where it hurts. I flop back down on the stairs and hide my face in my hands. "Hel's Realm."

I feel her sit next to me and turn to look at her. "Where do we go from here?"

She shakes her head. "I do not know, we are at an impasse. Neither of us is able to divulge everything they are privy to, the implications would be…" she holds her hands up, then lets them drop to her lap. "My oath to Sekhmet will not allow me to tell you everything that passes between gods, or vampires for that matter, and you cannot tell me what happens in the Sun King's inner circle. "

"Yeah, the first rule of god club, don't talk about god club."

She snorts. "Good analogy."

Chapter 43

Brunch is not where I expected to give my report. That said, I will enjoy every last bite of my mushroom omelette and every last sip of mimosa. The one good thing about hanging out with Var Royd is the food. You can always expect a five-star, gourmet meal, no skimping or fast food. Not that I don't enjoy the occasional burger from B-Bops, or swinging by Tasty Tacos when I'm out and about in the Metro.

"I will look into why the NTF is following you."

Ahh, the perks of being the Lord's Shadow—good food and protection from the authorities.

"You have done well."

The little voice in my head adds, Padawan, but is smart enough to keep it from slipping out. I doubt he'd understand, or find it humorous. "Umm, thanks."

"Will you be seeing him again?"

"Yeah, he has a benefit to attend this week and asked me to come along."

"Good, good." I'm waiting for the maniacal laughter and rubbing of hands, but he's seasoned enough to only let a gleam in his eyes show his excitement. "Remember to let me know what happens. Every detail."

Nodding, I set my fork down. Not even exotic mushrooms can make me pick it up again. This line of conversation makes me urn for flirtatious Var. Hel, I'd even take angry Var over creepy Var. Nothing like being whored out by your boss, or does this make him my pimp?

"Is your omelette not up to standards?"

"I'm full." Thanks to you, food is the last thing on my mind. I need a shower.

Var sets his napkin aside and stands, giving me high hopes this meeting is adjourned, only to have them stepped on with stilettos.

"There you are, late as ever." He embraces his twin.

I don't want to stand, but find myself at attention. It's not like she's queen of the elves, but she is a goddess. A bitchy goddess, but still a goddess, and I can fake respect with the best of them.

"Why be on time, or gods forbid early, when you can be fashionably late?" Turning toward me, her hundred watt smile dims to about twenty-five. "Keely."

"Vana." I really don't get what this woman has against me. I've done zip to her. Hel, I've done less than zip. Maybe it's because she prefers the company of men, not that I'd change my gender for an inkling of kindness. I'd settle for neutrality instead of being looked at like something stuck to the bottom of her Prada's, oh, I'm sorry Manolo Blahnik's. I may not be able to afford them, but I know a designer shoe when I see one.

"What a cute… outfit."

What a crock. She's judging my off-the-rack ensemble as if it were thrift store garbage. I've gotten some pretty sweet designer deals at thrift stores, so she can blow me. She can play the Mean Girl part all she wants, I refuse to let her bait me into playing her games. If beauty school taught me nothing else, it imparted the art of letting it roll off your back. It might make you feel better to blast them, but that feeling doesn't last and always comes back to bite you in the ass. Dealing with Vana Royd is no different, and she's got the firepower to do more than just make my life a living hel.

"Please, sit," she says, like she's doing us a favor by giving permission. "I can only stay a moment, I have to meet a friend."

"That friend wouldn't be Stasia Athory, would it?"

Twin sets of sea-and-sky-colored eyes turn toward me, Var's bright and curious, Vana's a rolling storm. Damn it, I said that with my outside voice. I cringe, wishing my chair would swallow me up and spit me out, back in my own apartment.

"Not that it is any of your business, but yes." Vana pushes away her place setting and holds her glass toward Var.

He fills it with mimosa, studying her as she takes a sip. "When did you and Miss Athory become friends?"

"We are not really friends, per say."

My spidey senses are all a tingle as I watch the volley between them. Unwittingly, I struck a match and the sparks are starting to take hold. To be more than honest, I'm just glad the heat is off me for the moment.

"If you are not *friends*, then what are you?"

"Business associates, if you must know."

Well, well, well, isn't that interesting. Two of the three women complicating my life have teamed up. I wonder what type of business they're conducting, besides finding new and inventive ways to harass and torment me. Then again, whatever they're up to could become another thorn in my side. But a thorn in my side is a thorn in Var's, and he's not going to let anything interfere with his plans. Better be nice to Var.

"Business associates." He rests his elbows on the table, steepling his fingers over his plate.

"Yes, business associates." Vana shrugs as she toys with her glass. "I have made a small investment in her company."

"I suppose I should not be surprised you

would be interested in the cosmetics industry."

"And what is wrong with the cosmetics industry? There is plenty of money to be made, ask your precious protege. She is hip deep in the beauty world."

Aww, shit, I knew it was too good to last. Both of them turn their attention my way, one wanting validation, the other… I don't know what he wants or expects me to say.

I do the only thing I can, agree. "She's right, on both counts. Male, female, En or Un, people will pay to look good. Especially, if it promises to turn back time, or make them look like the model in the advertisement."

Vana flashes me a smile, a genuine smile and I nearly fall off my chair.

"You have your insurance industry, why shouldn't I be allowed a hobby? Not that I need your permission."

His answer is a grunt, followed by a wave of his hand. "Fine, go play with your potions and lotions."

She stands, leaning in to drop a kiss on his cheek, before bouncing off like a happy little bunny. Playboy bunny, that is. Hel, maybe she gave Hef his start and influenced what the girls should look like. Wouldn't surprise me.

Var turns his attention to his abandoned plate and pushes it away. Guess his appetite is ruined too, can't say I'm sorry after he screwed with mine.

"This is probably for the best. It will make it easier for me to keep tabs on Miss Athory and remove her if she troubles you again."

I hadn't thought of it that way, but he's right. An inside man always makes things easier. An inside man. Damn it, the bitch didn't give up, she moved on. Since she can't get to me, Stasia is going to use Vana to get to Einen. That moves finding the key to the top of my to-do list.

Chapter 44

My building is as thick with mourning doves as my mind is with worthless plans to free Einen. Where do you find a key that isn't a key? Obviously, it's a magical lock, a normal lock wouldn't hold Vereinen. I need to figure out what Vana used to house the magic. Find the object and the key is mine to use as I see fit. I can use it to set him free, forget I ever found it, or I can move him to another location. Yeah, right, like I'm powerful enough to control him. Once he's out, he's going to stay out, there's no going back. And if everyone is right, that could be the beginning of the end. I still have my doubts. What to do, what to do.

Something thumps the top of my head as I unlock the door. I reach up to brush it away and my hand comes back wet, white, and disgusting. "Freakin' Hel!"

I glare up at the birds roosting above me. "You guys need to hit the road, sky, whatever, and tell your boss to leave me alone."

A strong hand pulls me to the side as another bomb hits the pavement. In my struggle to escape another splat hits the top of my sandaled foot.

"Damn it, Ric, don't sneak up on me like that."

He glances up at the birds. "It looks like your message has been ill received."

"No shit." A giant plop just misses me, splashing the sidewalk and door as I open it. "Or all the shit. Either way, get inside."

"Ladies first." Ric pushes me inside, following close enough I can feel the brush of leather against my bare legs.

"How do you stand it?"

"What? Bird droppings falling from your building?"

I stop mid-stair and turn to find him grinning at me. "No, silly, all that leather in ninety-something heat?"

He shrugs. "Heat does not bother me, cold on the other hand, is quite painful."

"Let me guess, it has something to do with you being a light elf, sorry, liosâlfar."

"Yes, and I am not Teiran. The term elf does not bother me. Although, he will be along shortly."

Pushing my apartment door open, we're treated to a screeching stream of cateese. I'm willing to bet my life it has something to do with Hel's minions. "Sorry, bud, I can't do anything about the birds, you're just going to have to ignore them."

"I have to agree with your feline. You do have a problem. Perhaps you should talk to her." Ric stands by the window seat, stroking CC's fur and studying the flock gathered on the sill.

"I'm tempted to call pest control, but it's not their fault, and I'll talk to her when I'm damn good and ready. I'm going to remove her *message*. Make yourself at home, I won't be long."

Is it wise to test the patience of a goddess? Probably not, but she needs to give me some space. In reality, I should get it over with. It won't be pleasant, but what is pleasant in my life at present? Besides, this bracelet needs to come off before something bad happens to my wrist. For all I know it's turning my skin a funny color, or breeding some kind of weird bacteria underneath.

I'm pulling my shirt into place when the bathroom door bangs against the wall, followed by a pile of paper thrust into my face. Woohoo, we go from one type of crap to another, Teiran's here and he's pissed. Nothing new there.

"Where did you get this?"

"Well, hello to you too." I grab the pile, skim the text and want to crawl down the drain with the bird doo-doo. Damn it, the print out from Mort detailing Ric's ordeal. How the hel did they find this? I must have left it sitting on the coffee table, that's what happens when you live alone. You become complacent and leave sensitive materials lying around.

"I asked you where you got these."

The beads of sweat on my upper lip have

nothing to do with the heat and humidity and everything to do with trying to find a graceful way out of this. "They were given to me."

"By who?"

"What were you doing snooping through my stuff? You're not my babysitter anymore. You don't live here, so you can't claim you were picking—

"I am not the one who found them."

His words lay across my shoulders like a thousand pound weight and I droop, clutching the sink for support. The person who lived it is the person who found it. My carelessness has opened old wounds that were never truly closed. I feel as shitty as the sidewalk outside my building. As punishment I should have to go out there and let Hel's fury rain down on me.

What's seen can't be unseen, but what do I do about it? Come clean and tell them about Mort, or try and BS my way out of it, with an anonymous sender story? Looking up at the mirror, I see Teiran has left, probably fed up with waiting for an answer. I can't hide in the bathroom forever, no matter how much I'd like to. Hel, right now anything sounds better than taking one step into my living room. Facing Ric alone is bad, beyond bad, but both of them waiting for an explanation makes the thought of visiting a pissed off goddess of the underworld sound good.

A stiletto stomps on my chest, the heel grinding

in, as I meet Ric's eyes. The rawness of his pain rips me apart. I would subject myself to any amount of torture to erase those words he read. Even if it meant having to wear the collar for eternity.

"I'm sorry… you weren't meant to see those."

His voice is barely above a whisper, "Where did you get them?"

I open my mouth, but one glance at Teiran tears the lie from my lips before it reaches fruition. "Remember the man in tweed, the one I ran into in the skywalk, spilling his coffee?"

They both nod.

"His name is Mortonson, but likes to be called Mort."

Teiran makes a rolling gesture with his hand and it's all I can do to keep from telling him to give it a rest.

"That meeting wasn't a coincidence, he's been following me."

"Why?" Ric slides to the edge of the couch, his own problems forgotten as Sword mode kicks into play. Now I really feel like crap, it's just like him to push aside his own feelings with the possibility of me being in danger.

"He wants to study me."

Teiran's gaze narrows. "Study you? Because of your Talents?"

I briefly acknowledge Teiran's questions with a nod. "It seems his family has been studying my kind for a while now and he's taken up where they left off. His great-grandfather was part of the Ahnenerbe Society."

Chapter 45

You'd swear I dropped a bomb obliterating the power of speech. I really wish someone would say something, anything. Even the cat stops bird-watching and focuses on me after those two little words.

"I knew better than to trust you. First Vereinen, then Hel, and now this, how could you side with one of the greatest evils?"

Teiran's words sting more than they should. It's not the first time he's pointed out his lack of trust, but this is uncalled for, I thought he knew me better. "You've made it abundantly clear you're not thrilled about having to work with me."

Foolishly, I find myself standing a hairsbreadth from him. When he opens his mouth I give him a shove. "Shut it, Teiran, I'm not finished. I would never align myself with a Nazi organization."

"Keely—"

It's hard to be mad at Ric, he's the one who was hurt by my actions, but it doesn't stop me from shooting him a warning glance to stay out of it. Holding up his hands in concession, he steps away from us.

My confidence grows as Teiran's eyes widen, and I plant a finger against his chest. "I haven't *sided* with Hel or Einen. And since you brought up trust, let's talk about how after you took it off, you shoved my collar in your pocket. If we're going to work together, I have to know you have my back. I saw you put the collar in your pocket, that doesn't exactly inspire trust. Bet you carry it everywhere. Hel, I'd be willing to stake my life, it's there right now."

Well, lookie there, little ol' me made the Big Bad Wolf take a step back.

"Is this true?" Ric's voice may be soft, but it holds a surprising edge.

Teiran's yes is a long, drawn-out hissing sigh. "I hold it because there may come a time when she loses control, like the other..."

"How many times to do I have to tell you, I'm not Einen?" Hanging my head, I walk away and sit on the edge of the couch. "I don't even know what he did that was so bad. The only thing I've been told is that he tried to overthrow Var, end of subject move on. If you guys don't tell me what he did, how am I supposed to keep from repeating it?"

Ric sits next to me, placing a hand on my thigh. "I am sorry, Keely. It is unfair of us to expect you to understand without explanation."

"No, it's me who should be sorry. I should have brought those papers to you right away, I just didn't know how to broach the subject without hurting you. That's the last thing I want to do." I glance up at Teiran. "No matter how much you hate and distrust me, Teiran, hurting either of you is not on my bucket list."

I may have chipped away a portion of the rage and mistrust, but when our eyes meet, the shadow of doubt still clings to Teiran. Whatever Einen did, it goes much deeper with Teiran than Ric and I have no idea how to move past it, with the exception of removing my Talents. If that were possible, neither of them would be in my life and I'm not sure if that's a good or a bad thing. Strange how a confrontation can make you realize you actually care about someone.

Ric pats my leg, chasing away any stray, off topic thoughts. "Tell us more about this Mort."

"He's bookish, wears a tweed suit like it's a uniform, claims he and his family are not Nazis, and keeps showing up when I least expect him. It makes me wonder if he's got the fever."

"I suppose that is a possibility. Has he told you anything of value?"

I glance at the papers still clutched in my fist.

"About you and your Talents?"

"Yeah, he says I'm not a necromancer."

Puzzled looks pass between them, Teiran opens his mouth, closes it, opens it again then shakes his head. Probably deciding it's better that Ric continue questioning me. Can't say I'm opposed.

"What about your powers over the dead?"

"He said necromancy is used to communicate with the dead, not control them. What I do is called necrokinesis, since I can control them. And something about what I am—half light, half dark—allows me to control things in the in-between state, like vamps since they aren't dead or alive."

I can damn near see the lightbulbs click on above their heads, an eagerness to know more shining in their eyes. Hope they're taking notes, because Var is going to be giving them a pop quiz when he finds out. Aw, hel, I didn't even add the Var factor into this equation.

"Is there anything else you can share?"

"Not really, and not because I don't want to," I quickly add, seeing Teiran ready to question my loyalty once again. "It's because I've blown him off, the whole Ahnenerbe, Nazi thing creeps me out. And what he gave me was enough for me to do a little cyber hunting. Hold on a second."

I knew printing out those webpages would be beneficial. Grabbing them from the office, I hurry back, the soft conversation between them stopping as I enter the room. My raised brows and what-did-we-just-say-about-trust look are totally blown off as they grab the sheets and begin reading.

"You do realize this is all based on fiction and video games."

Freakin' Teiran thinks he's so smart. "Duh, but all fiction is based on fact. Take a look in the mirror."

There's a choking sound to my right, egging me on. I smile and bat my lashes at Teiran, who scowls at both of us.

"Shadowkinesis looks very promising." Ric passes a page to Teiran and he nods after skimming.

"That's what I thought, but how do we find out more?"

They both look at me as if I've grown a second head.

Teiran's smile leans toward malicious. "We, or I should say you, call on your friend, Mort. He seems to want to give you the answers, I vote we let him. Do not worry, we *have your back.*"

Isn't it grand when your own words come back to haunt you?

Chapter 46

Since Mort already has my home number, it's decided I'll use it to contact him. No use giving him another way to contact me by revealing my cell number. Fun fact, unlisted numbers aren't truly unlisted, and in this case Google, or the public record search he must have used, was not my friend.

I flip the card he gave me through my fingers, hoping the knots in my stomach will loosen before I dial. I'm not really as scared of him as much as I'm scared of what Teiran will do to him. And there's the possibility Ric will come unglued about the info he passed to me. The kid may creep me out, but he doesn't deserve the full wrath of either of them, even if it is only a possibility.

Speaking of wrath, Teiran hands me the receiver. "Make the call."

Choking back the butterflies that threaten to escape, I dial the number. After the third ring, my load lightens. I can hang up at four, right? Three rings is all it takes.

"Hello, Miss Fey." An over-excited voice punctuates that third ring.

It still creeps me out that he has my home

number. "Hi, Mort, can you meet me at Midnite Expresso? We'd li—we need to talk."

"Of course I can, what time?"

Luck must be with me in some shape or form, the overly-eager beaver didn't even notice I'd nearly blown Teiran and Ric's plan. But Teiran did, and lets me know about it with a hand to the shoulder, that includes constricting fingers.

"When can you be there?"

"I'll leave right away, I'm staying in Perry, so about fifteen minutes?"

"Perfect, see you in fifteen." I hang up the phone and pull myself from Teiran's grasp. "Geez dude, that hurts."

"It was meant to, your lack of thought almost ruined everything."

"Did not, he didn't even notice."

"You were lucky, but your slip of the tongue solidifies the fact that Ric and I shall be the ones doing the talking when we meet your friend."

"For the last time, he's not my friend." *Any more than you are at the moment.*

Ric reaches for the doorknob. "We should get there before he does, I want to make sure we're seated out of sight when he arrives."

"Fine, let me grab my purse and we'll go." Slinging my bag over my shoulder, I walk out and wait for them to exit. They in turn wait for me to finish locking the door, that whole ladies first thing. Not that I mind, it's kind of refreshing to be treated with a little respect, even if it is because of my gender and not who and what I am.

Deep down, I know I could command respect by showing what I am, but who wants to have to take something that should be given? Although, a show of strength might be what I need to get more than polite respect from Teiran. But do I want to cross that line?

Ric holds the door of Midnite Expresso, but Teiran enters first, looks around, then waves us in. Being part of such a tactical team is weird and unnatural feeling. I don't know how to act or react, no matter how many times they go over it in training. I mean, we're just going for coffee, coffee with a card-holding member of a secret Nazi society. It doesn't matter the Tweed keeps telling me he's not a Nazi, or that his great grandpappy wasn't a Nazi, it still skeeves me out. I dare anyone to not to be freaked by possible connections to the group.

"You sit here, where he can see you when he enters." Teiran directs me to a table in the middle of the room. "We will be over there, where we can see but remain unseen." He nods to a table by the bathrooms, the same table we've used as a trio.

"Can I get something to drink first?"

"Alric is taking care of you beverage."

I glance over at the counter, Candy holds up

three spread fingers, then rounds her hand into a C shape and I nod. My usual, a white chocolate mocha. I hear the shuffle of ice and smile. Leave it to Candy to remember I drink my WC chilled in the summer.

Fingers snap in front of my face and I jump, scowling at the owner of those fingers. "Pay attention. You will sit here."

He pulls out the chair that faces the wall, with the counter behind me, and a view of the door to my left. I'm not thrilled with the positioning, it leaves me exposed on all sides. It would be more comforting if I could face the counter. Maybe I am learning something from my training.

"Make sure he sits across from you, or beside you with his back to us."

"I suppose you want me to keep him from getting a drink too."

"No, we can keep him from seeing us."

"What about if he has to use the bathroom?"

His lids drop as a breath of frustration is pushed from his lips.

"Come on, it's a legitimate question."

"One you do not need to worry about."

"Whatever." I sit, putting my phone on the table, and stuff my purse onto the chair on my left. Teiran nods in approval, no one would move a woman's purse to sit down, not without asking.

Ric places a napkin on the table followed by

my drink, condensation already gathering on the glass. That tells you how hot it is today, everything sweats, even in an artificially cooled environment. "Relax, we will be watching and step in when the time is right."

I nod, my smile wavering. "I know, but it doesn't stop me from being nervous. I'm not exactly cut out for this type of work."

"Think of it as an interview. You are in control, not the person you are interviewing."

I nod again, catching a glimpse of brown tweed out of the corner of my eye. "You better skedaddle, he's here."

With a pat to the shoulder, he and Teiran make their way to the back of the room. Why is it, the thought of them being next to the bathroom suddenly makes me have to go?

The bell rings and I half-stand, waving Mort over.

"Miss Fey, I'm so glad you called."

"Hi, Mort, have a seat." I motion to the chair across from me. Yes, the chair next to me would be a better choice when talking over sensitive material, but I don't want him that close to me.

"Do you mind if I grab something to drink first?"

"Nope, go for it." The whole thirty-seconds he's at the counter, it's a fight not to glance in the direction of my partners. I imagine Teiran would be pretty pissed if I gave them away, Ric probably wouldn't be very happy either.

Mort is back with a steaming cup and a grin that would light The Meadows. "I'm so happy you called."

I manage to hold back a little sigh of relief when he sits in the appropriate seat. "Yeah, you said that."

He takes a sip from his cup. "My, that's exceptional coffee."

"Candy knows her stuff, but that's not why I called." I tap the button my phone. "I don't have a lot of time, what else can you tell me about what I am?"

Sliding his cup to the side, he lays a briefcase that dates back to the 1950's on the table and shuffles through some papers. With his clothing and accessory choices, I'm stating to wonder if Mort was born in the wrong century.

"Here we are." He hands me a hefty file labeled *Schattenkind*. I'm quite curious to know what else is in that case, but I'll leave that to the boys. I have what I came for and getting it was easier than I thought.

Chapter 47

Once I have written proof in my hand, there's no need for me to continue this farce of an *interview*. Hel, I don't need to have any contact with Mort, he just made himself completely obsolete. I turn toward the back of the room and nod.

Ric reaches us first, vamp speed comes in handy, and takes the seat to my left. Leaving Teiran to cover my right flank. Poor, Mort, I almost feel sorry for him. I'm not sure of his true intentions toward me, or what he expected to get out of this meeting, but being sandwiched by the Sword and Shield certainly wasn't part of his plan.

"Mort, meet Ric and Teiran, also known—"

"The Sword and the Shield, a pleasure to meet you both." His fear is quickly overtaken with curiosity. He's on his feet, hand extended to Ric and then Teiran, who true to form refuses to acknowledge the gesture. Hurt? Annoyed? Maybe a little fear returning, Mort retracts his hand and sits.

"Miss Fey tells us you have information about her Talents, Mr. Mortonson." It was decide Ric would handle chatting up Mort. A variation of good cop, bad cop, that isn't hard for Mort to pick up on. Especially, with Teiran doing what he does best, intimidation.

Mort nods, and Ric's warm-and-friendly smile counter acts Teiran's ready-to-rip-your-throat-out glare. The projection of friendliness surprises me a bit. Deep down, Ric has to be livid about the files Mort passed to me.

"Yes, I just gave her most of it."

What the—most of it? Damn little sneak. I've only got myself to blame, should have known he wouldn't give me everything. If I were in his shoes, I would have done the same.

"She also told us, you belong to the Ahnenerbe Society."

Mort's glasses bounce on his nose as his head bobs fanatically. "Yes, sir, I do."

"The group has been silent for so long, it surprised me to hear they still exist."

"After the fall of the Nazi party, they—we—went underground. The stigma of association gave us a bad name."

Teiran snorts. "I should say so."

Mort's lips part, his features indignant, but a gesture from Ric pulls his attention away.

I punch Teiran in the thigh and he grabs my hand, holding it firmly under the table. His expression screaming, 'never do that again.' But you know what? I'd do it again in a heartbeat. If he screws up my finding out about what I am because of his temper, I'll take a piece out of him myself.

"Currently, no one knows who we are, or what we do. But they didn't truly understand what the Ahnenerbe did in the past either." Mort takes a sip from his mug, an air of vindication flowing off of him.

The little shit really believes the crap he spouts. I doubt he *truly* understands who they were or what they did either. I'm not saying I know, but when you see from several sources that the group was the brain child of Heinrich Himmler, you know it can't be rainbows and unicorns. Then again, I bet there's a file in that case labeled unicorns and another about harnessing the power of rainbows.

My fingers are starting to fall asleep under the pressure of Teiran's grasp. I wiggle them, failing to break his hold, but he does loosen it slightly. Glancing over at him, he raises a challenging brow. Nope, not gonna bite. I smile sweetly and bat my lashes until he frowns, then turn back to Ric and Mort's discussion.

"Would you be willing to share the Ahnenerbe's knowledge?"

"That depends on the information you want, I don't have access to everything. Some things are off limits, I'm just a clerk after all."

"We were lead to believe you held a higher position."

Again the little turd duped me. Making me

think he was something he isn't, or maybe I just made assumptions. I guess that's possible, he never did tell me what he did. His confidence, the way he dressed, and the bits and pieces he told me about led me to believe he held a higher position. You know what they say about assuming…

Mort turns an earnest, open face toward me. "I'm sorry, Miss Fey, if I led you to believe otherwise. I'm working toward becoming a researcher, and finding you was a step in that direction."

All I can do is nod. Words escape me, appropriate words that is. I can find all kinds of words to express my irritation and disappointment with the turn of events. Teiran's thumb draws a slow circle on my palm. Lost in my private pity party, I'd forgotten his hold on me. The sensation is part reassuring, as if he knows my disappointment, and part sensual, like he's forgotten where we are. I look at him from under my lashes, but he's concentrating on Ric and Mort. It's possible he doesn't even know he's doing it. Then again, when does Teiran do anything he's not fully aware of? It feels… nice, so I'm not complaining.

"The files you gave Miss Fey could be accessed by anyone in your organization?"

Mort avoids eye contact, his mouth imitating a fish. "Not exactly, I sort of made copies without anyone knowing."

Ric takes turns looking from me to Teiran.

He's not projecting anything so I'm not exactly sure where this is going, but if I'm reading his expression correctly, I think Mort's in for a big surprise.

"How did you gain access if you did not have clearance?"

"Part of my job as clerk is to file things, that's how I knew they were there. When it was decided to digitize the files, I was placed on the team to make the conversions. That's when I made the copies."

That means someone has been looking at the schattenkind files recently. Is the Ahnenerbe thinking about paying me an official visit? After all, Mort was an unofficial one.

Chapter 48

Our regularly scheduled training session has been interrupted by this important message: We have files on the schattenkind. It's like every holiday wrapped up into one little file folder and you can't wait to tear into it, at least I can't. Lucky for me, neither can my training team.

Three half-eaten pizzas and several bottles of beer, in various states from full to empty, litter my kitchen. Everyone is so engrossed in our reading material that food and drink are secondary, only needed to fuel this all-nighter. For two of us, anyway. Ric and Dara may enjoy the flavors and scents, but they don't need this type of sustenance. It's just a pleasure thing for them. While Teiran and I need food, the alcohol is a celebratory treat.

There's a lot we already know, but the fact that the Ahnenerbe Society put so much work into this, makes me a little nervous. What if they decide to start up their experimentation again? With Einen out of the picture, I move up to subject number one. I don't want to end up on the slides under the microscope. I know my team will do their best to keep me safe, but what if the Ahnenerbe decide they need to be studied too. Hel, Ric's already been on the receiving end of their perversion of science. Imagine what they'd do to Teiran with his helhound side and ability to control the dark, or Dara. With her ties to Sekhmet, I bet they'd love to get their grubby little hands on her.

"Keely, your research on those websites was correct." Ric passes me a page.

"Shadowkinesis, the ability to shape and manipulate shadows. Told ya, all fiction is based in fact." I've never shaped one before, that will be up next in shadow play. I stick my tongue out at Teiran.

He doesn't even look up from his reading. "Your face will stick like that."

"How would you know, you can't even see what I'm doing."

"I know because it is what I expect of you, something childish and immature."

I blow raspberries, and am rewarded with a snort from Dara and a chuckle from Ric. Even Dara has a better sense of humor than Teiran. Hel, most of the time I question if he has one at all.

"You should cut her some slack, Teiran. Technically, she is a child."

As proud as I am of Ric for attempting slang, I'm not sure I like being called a child. Even if I am practically a baby when you look at the ages of those in the room with me. Although being called a kid is better than having someone call you ma'am. Nothing makes you feel like a middle-aged woman more than hearing that word.

"Teiran," says Dara, holding out a page. "This will be of personal interest to you."

I wonder if it has something to do with that other thing I found, umber, umbra something or other. Maybe then he'd put a little more credence into my fiction-breeding-fact theory. As he skims the contents, his expression changes faster than Rey changes girlfriends. Whatever's on the page it isn't what I thought it was, there's no way giving a name to his Talent would push him to whatever it is he's feeling. Fear? Rage? A combination of the two?

He crumples the page and tosses it across the room, quickly following to snatch it up before any of us can. Face grim, he nearly pulls the door from its hinges, rattling it in its frame on his way out.

Dara shakes her head as Ric and I turn toward her. "If he wants to tell you, that is his business."

What the—Cat Woman is sticking up for the Big Bad Wolf?

The couch moves beside me as Ric stands, concern written in red ink all over his face. "I should go see if he is all right. You two can keep reading."

Once the door is shut, I turn to Dara. "You're seriously not going to say anything?"

She shakes her head, not even looking up from the next sheet.

Every bone is vibrating with curiosity. I wish he wouldn't have taken the paper with him. "Come on, not one little clue?"

"No, Nosey Nelly, get back to reading."

"But you don't even like Teiran."

Head held high, she looks down her nose at me. "While I may not *like* him, I respect him, and that respect extends to keeping his secrets. They are his to tell. Worry less about his problems and more about your own, you sound like Nyssa."

Cringing, I reach for the pages Ric abandoned. Dara's right, no matter how much I'm dying to know, it doesn't concern me. On the other hand, considering we work together, anything in this file could impact any of us. I hope he takes our trust chat to heart and confides in us if it's something that could endanger our triad, or anyone else connected to us.

What the hel am I saying? I'm worse than a gossipy Nyssa. I have no business bitching about people keeping things from me. I've kept too many secrets that could endanger everyone around me. The first file Mort gave me. The debt I owe Hel. My visits to Einen. Hel's Realm, I'm the poster child of untrustworthiness.

I've got to stop blaming my situation on every secret kept by someone else. True, some of them could have helped me out of, or prepared me for, my currant predicament, but not all secrets are detrimental to me and my survival.

"This is all interesting, but without context and proof, it is nothing but speculation." Dara stacks her pages neatly back into the folder.

"It's nothing but guesswork." I gather the rest of the pages and add them to the others. "But it's a starting point. I just need to figure out if I'm capable of doing these things."

"I suggest starting slowly and with supervision."

I nod, Teiran's control over the dark and Ric's blinding sword might be the antidote I need if things go south. Then again, if things go too far south, like South Pole south, Dara may have to carry out Sekhmet's orders and finish me.

Chapter 49

"You've got to be shitting me." Dealing with a compliance letter from the city is the last thing I need in my overflowing schedule. I hand the letter back to Win and Rey snags it mid handover.

"Well, considering the subject is shit… " He shrugs, holding it back out to me.

Nyssa grabs the letter and shakes her head. "What do they expect you to do about the bird problem? Pest control isn't on our list of services."

Win takes the letter from Nyssa, putting it neatly back into its envelope. "Would you like me to send this over to Mr. Royd?"

"No, I'll handle it." The last thing I need is to be running to Var every time something goes wrong, even if it is tempting.

"Would you like me to call an exterminator?"

"Thanks, Win, but I'll deal with the problem." An exterminator isn't going to be able to do squat. There's only one way to make this stop and I can't keep putting it off. I have to go talk to the Queen of Helheim. "Do you guys think you can hold down the fort for a couple of hours, while I handle this?"

"Sure, Boss," says Rey with a wicked grin. "Do

you think we should breakout the umbrellas for our clients?"

Take back everything I said, the last thing I need is Rey's smart mouth. "And on that note, Win, I'm leaving you in charge."

"Hey, why Win? I know the Fox isn't capable, but what about me?"

"You're in charge of keeping the Fox in line, Nys."

With laughter from Rey, an efficient nod from Win, and happy childlike bouncing from Nyssa, I head upstairs. My feet feel encased in slow drying cement, each step harder to make, as I contemplate facing Hel. This meeting can go only one way. Badly.

I'd rather have tea with Vana and Stasia, than deal with Hel. She's not happy with me, proven by the literal shit storm outside my building. And I have to take off my only defense against her to have this meeting. Even I have to admit, this is one of those times I *need* some backup. Someone to watch over me, and if things turn for the worst—as I imagine they will—slam the bracelet back on my wrist.

My choices are many, but there are very few I'd trust—no, that's not the right word, I'd *ask* to take on this task. I'd never involve my crew downstairs, it's not that I don't think they'd do it, it's more along the lines of keeping them out of this mess.

Like the others, I refuse to get Mel tangled up in this. Dara's asleep. Annya's too far away. Var doesn't know anything about my dealings with Hel and I want to keep it that way. That leaves Ric and Teiran.

Scrolling through the contacts list on my phone, my finger wavers over their names. I only need one of them. Ric would go along with my plan, reluctantly, but he'd understand. Teiran would fight me every step of the way. My finger taps the logical choice.

I am unable to answer at present, please leave a message…

Oh, crappy day, he's probably on some mundane chore for Var. No telling how long it will take, or if he'll get back to me in time. I tap the little hang-up button before the beep. He'll still know I called, but why bother with a message when it will be too late?

My finger hovers over Teiran's name, I know with all my heart I'll regret this, but he's better than nothing. The worst thing he can say is no, leaving me to get by on my wit and charm. Not my preferred method when dealing with Hel. Here goes nothing, or everything, depending on how you look at it.

"What do you want, Shadow?"

"You."

If the silence on the other end doesn't remind

me why I should think before opening my mouth, his quick intake of breath does. I am so glad he can't see the fifty shades of red my cheeks take on.

"When, where, and for what purpose?"

"Now, my apartment, and not for whatever you're thinking."

"I was not thinking of anything in particular."

I so want to argue the point, but it will only lead to my embarrassment. Not to mention, piss him off, if I do that he definitely won't help me. "Look, I need your help."

"In what capacity?"

"Backup, I have to go talk to Hel."

Silence again.

"I need you to put my bracelet back on if things go badly."

More silence. I'm getting the feeling he wants me to beg. If that's what it takes, then so be it, I'll beg. "Seriously, Teiran, I need your help. I can't do this alone."

Time slows as I listen to the sounds of silence on the other side and I begin to wonder if I've lost my connection. Cell service is touch and go in The Meadows and he's out in the boonies. A big whoppin' fifteen minutes away, but still considered the middle of nowhere by city dweller standards.

"Teiran?"

"I will be there in twenty." He hangs up before I can even form the word thank and you is lost in the moment as of relief washes over me. Reluctant or not, I have backup.

Now, I just have to worry about what I'm going to say to Hel to get her to stop the biohazard blizzard outside my building.

Chapter 50

I lay on the couch, my head in his lap. One of his hands holds my arm, the other clasps the bracelet. It's far too intimate for comfort, but he insists it's the best way for him to control the situation. Settling on a signal for 'get me out' was much harder.

Once I've sent my subconscious into her realm, I don't think we'll be able to communicate. I'm going to have to trust him to monitor my vitals and bodily actions. If she inflicts any harm, I'm counting on it showing up physically. In reality, I have no idea what will happen. As a counter measure, it was decided if I'm gone longer than twenty minutes, he'll slap the bracelet into place and pull me out. Twenty minutes sounds like a lifetime when you're making a trip to hel.

Eyes closed, I take a deep breath and begin at my toes, concentrating on relaxing every muscle. When my feet feel as if they will float away, I move upward and, somewhere around my waist, I find myself deep within the dank mist of Niflheim. In the distance I see the border of Helheim and its mistress.

Before I can wonder if Teiran managed to set the timer, a pain brightens my vision and rings in my ears. Raising a hand to my cheek, feel the sting of cold, not heat, where her hand connected. The bitch slapped me.

"That was too light of a punishment, when I count the ways you have defied me."

"I didn't mean to ignore you. I had my reasons."

"Those reasons are the only thing keeping me from extracting a higher, more pain-filled payment. The slap was but a reminder that I do not tolerate defiance."

At least Var didn't smack me around when I ignored his calls. Seems she knows what I've been up to without me reporting in. It makes me wonder if she has more spies than just the mourning doves.

"How is it you are able to reject my call?"

"Willpower?" I flinch as she raises her hand. Sometimes white lies and half-truths are lifesavers. "I apologize, but in all seriousness, I don't understand how I'm able to avoid our talks."

See? Half-truth, I know the bracelet works, but I don't know how. I try focusing on the living side of her scowl, but ignoring the dead and decaying side is like trying to keep from gawking at an accident.

Something tells me she's not buying it, so I do what anyone would in this situation, I throw someone under the bus. "Could it be something

Var's doing? Blocking you from contacting me?"

Her anger wavers as she contemplates Var's hand in keeping me from her. "It is possible."

I fight the urge to shiver as her gravel-coated voice rakes my spine. I bite the inside of my cheek to keep from showing anything that might be misconstrued as lying. Fear she doesn't mind, but if she sniffs a lie, well… let's hope Teiran can slap that bracelet on fast enough. For now it looks as if she's buying my excuses.

"But if that were true, how is it you are here now?"

Or not.

"Maybe my need to see you helped?"

"So tell me, little Schattenkind, why this sudden need to see me?"

"To let you know I've been practicing my spying techniques and Var is pleased. I think he's starting to trust me." I'm quite proud of myself for not blurting out my assignment to watch Haydn Koehler.

She nods, bits of dead and dying skin flap, and a tooth falls from her lipless side into the mist at our feet. I damn near feel sorry for her, since it must suck to be stuck in a never-ending cycle of falling apart at the seams. There is a remedy for her condition. Me. If I touch her, she becomes whole, in a matter of speaking. One side turns to crystal, the other obsidian, and she's breathtakingly beautiful. So beautiful it hurts. Part of me wonders if that's her end game, figuring out a way to make that change permanent. Add that little nugget to the things to fear list.

"Is that the only reason you have graced me with your presence?"

"No, unfortunately, the birds you've placed outside my building are causing a problem."

Her laughter is almost worse than her speaking voice, a cross between a smoker's hack and the sweet laughter of a child.

"They're drawing unwanted attention. Both Teiran and Ric are wondering why your mourning doves are hanging around. I'm worried they'll take the info to Var."

"I shall remove them." She turns her empty eye socket toward me.

It's not like I did a touchdown dance, but my excitement must be showing.

"Most of them, on the condition you do whatever it is you did today and continue to report your advancement with Ingvar."

The ground quakes, or maybe it's just me. She's standing as still as the air, but her form begins to fade, along with the dank, misty landscape. With a blink of her one good eye, I'm staring at Teiran's wavering face.

I push his insistent hands away. "Stop shaking me, or I'm gonna toss my cookies."

He gently helps me sit up and I feel my wrist. The bracelet's back where it belongs. "It worked, hallelujah."

"What did she want?"

"She was pissed because I've been avoiding her." His raised brow signals he already knew that and wants more, but I can't give him everything. If he knew I was double agenting it, he'd… well, who knows what he'd do? "But I got her to get rid of most of the birds littering my sidewalk, and that means the City Council will get off my back."

"Getting rid of the birds was why you needed to meet with her?"

I just totally blew my little white lie of her showing up unannounced, playing off the parking garage incident with Ric. I'm so glad I didn't tell him the real reason before we started. He would have never agreed to help me. As it is, he's going to be pissed at me for a long, long time. Gods help me when I need someone to play bracelet backup. On the bright side, I won't be needing that kind of help for a while. At least not until Hel rains on my parade again.

Chapter 51

After the stress of the compliance letter, a meeting with Hel, and a steady stream of the three C's—cut, color, and curl—I'm tired. But not so tired I can forget about fitting in another chat with Shadow Copy. Matter of fact, the thought energizes me, when coupled with a strong pot of black coffee. No milk or cream, no frou-frou sugary mixtures, just straight up caffeine. Lordy, am I gonna crash after this and it's not going to be pretty.

SC knew a little more than Einen about his prison—not surprising, since he was on the outside—but the visions he shared were blurry to the point of nothing more than three or four black blobs, hanging out around Einen's bedroom door. I mark it up to lack of experience and I'd already extended myself when he stepped forward to help. Extended, what an understatement. I'd had total shield failure. I did manage to pull it together in the end. Success. Guess they cancel each other out, leaving me with a *learning experience*. Now that I have a better idea of what to expect, I might be able to make heads or tails out of what he shows me.

Each time I travel or border hop, whatever

you want to call it, it gets a little easier. Visiting Hel isn't tricky, probably because of the mark she embroidered into my wrist, a combination of the runes Ear and Berkana. Einen's place is the easiest, he'd explained it as 'like calling to like,' in other words because of our genetic makeup. I think it helped that he began appearing to me at a young age, masquerading as my imaginary friend. He had to have been grooming me for the future with our fantastical adventures. As I matured, it all dissipated into a hazy memory, the block The Sisters and Mel put on my Talents had a hand in that.

The worst part of this type of traveling is leaving my body unattended and vulnerable. Sure, I have locks and wards on my building and CC is an awesome body watcher, but there's always that niggling fear in the back of my brain. What if someone found my body? If they destroyed it, would it leave me in limbo or kill me? Neither option is appealing. Having a sit-down with Annya to discuss all things out of body travel might be a good idea. She's a pro with both dream walking and border hopping.

Var's words come back to haunt me, *use the tools you have*. I prefer to think of it as asking for assistance—something I have a difficult time doing—instead of *using* people. And I really hate that he thinks of us as *tools* and not living, breathing entities, with our own wants and desires. Gotta get used to dealing with gods and their way of thinking, because I'll never make them see it differently.

Holding visions of Einen's house in my mind, I begin the relaxation techniques, staring with my toes, working my way up. I've never gotten beyond my waist and this time is no different, at about the kneecap, I'm under and gone.

The once vibrantly colored lawns and gardens turned grey scale, are even more desolate than my last visit. Grass crunches underfoot and foliage turns to dust when touched. No sounds or movement, besides those I make and the beating of my own pulse in my ears. You'd think there would be something, but there's nothing, not even the swish and crackle underfoot.

Einen's opulent mansion is a horror movie's dream. Most of the windows are broken, and one of the front doors dangles from its hinges. The front steps are treacherous, cracked and crumbling under my feet. The stone has lost all its luster and I'm afraid to touch it, fearful it too will crumble. Hel, I'm afraid to go inside, the whole thing might come down if disturbed.

Is all of this a result of Vana's spells? Or Einen's imprisonment? Is there some tie between his wellbeing and the condition of his home?

My first instinct is to run upstairs and check on Einen, but the tingle at the base of my skull keeps me from entering the house. I need to find Shadow Copy, he might be able to clue me in on what's happening, but that means I have to enter. With each step toward the doors, the tingle intensifies. By the time I'm standing at the entrance, my whole body feels overrun with invisible creepy crawlies.

Everything about my situation screams, *run, wake up, get back to your body*, but the ridiculous notion that Einen is my friend keeps me rooted in place. If I can't force myself to go in, maybe I can send in a shadow or two, or reach out to those inside. Use the tools at my disposal, instead of placing my own hide in harm's way. Remembering the pain they felt when I used them to find Einen makes it difficult to see them as tools. In their own way, they are as alive as any creature. But when push comes to shove, I have to look past that and call on them to do what I can't or won't.

The biggest shadow should come from the house, but there's nothing. Maybe it's the position of whatever lights this place, and the shadow is at the back of the house. That doesn't make any sense, there should still be shadows. I spin around searching the porch, the grounds, but there are no shadows, anywhere. What the...

My own shadow's nonexistence is the final kick in the ass I need to send me packing.

I lay in bed, unable to fathom what I witnessed. The absolute absence of shadow, at least as far as

I'd seen, but I'd been too chicken to go inside. I'd just been there a couple of days ago and it hadn't been this bad, this… flat and empty. Sure, things had been dying, but I assumed it was lack of care. Now, it's as if *all* the life has been sucked out of it, reducing it to… nothingness. No sound, no movement, nothing except that insane feeling of repulsion.

Damn it, have I been duped into believing an illusion or glamour?

Chapter 52

Haydn sets down his fork, steeples his hands under his chin and studies me. "Am I boring you?"

"No, it's not you—"

"It's me. You do realize it's always them and never you, right?" His smirk is contagious. "There's the smile I've been looking for."

"Sorry, I've been so preoccupied."

"Work's a bitch, especially when you have to take time out of your day to have dinner with it." He winks at me.

"Even I have to admit, having dinner with you doesn't constitute work. You've made my job entirely too easy." So easy, I'm still waiting for the catch. There's always a catch, usually ending in someone wanting something from me. From wanting me to work as their spy to wanting an actual piece of me.

"The only person I want things to be difficult for is your boss."

"You've made that pretty clear, I just don't know how I can help you."

His laughter stirs up high school memories, of John Taylor's base vibrating the car seats as we circled the loop. A friend referred to it as pussy thumping base. If you need an explanation, you probably aren't meant to understand. And if you don't know what a loop is, you're probably too young to be worrying about that part of the female anatomy.

"Your mere presence at my side helps me."

Yeah, it screams, hey Var, I've got your toy. Call me cynical, but I've learned there are very few I can trust, and even in that small group it's to varying degrees. "You know me, always willing to help."

"No, actually, I don't, but I'd like to. In fact, I'd like to help you."

"You're already letting me follow you around to keep Var off my back, what more could I ask for?"

"I know there's something you're looking for, maybe I can help you find it."

Not a big secret I'm searching for info about what I am, but what could he possibly tell me that I haven't learned already? It doesn't take a reporter to figure that out. "Are you proposing I put an ad in your paper?" I try to lighten the sarcasm with a smile and light tone.

"Not quite what I was getting at, but if you did want to advertise your salon…"

I echo his laughter and shake my head. "No thanks, we're busy enough as it is. I wouldn't have time for anything else."

"Well we can't have that. You'd never have time to shadow me." He winks at me then motions to the server. "Dessert? They make the best damn bread pudding, smothered in caramel sauce and topped with ice cream."

My mouth waters at the thought, but stereotypical female dessert shame kicks in and I shrug.

"Oh, come on. Don't tell me you're one of those, 'I'm watching my weight,' type of girls?"

I shake my head. It was pretty evident by my clean plate I'm not watching my weight and it wasn't a salad I'd devoured. It has nothing to do with watching my weight, more along the lines of not wanting to look like a complete pig.

"Fine, it's settled, we'll share." He turns to the waitress, flipping on the boyish charm. "One bread pudding, two spoons."

She grins back, brushing against him as she clears our plates. Wow, what is it with the guys I hang out with? They're all sexual magnets. Glancing up, I see Haydn studying me, a slow smile tugging at his lips. Unholy crap, does he take my watching the waitress as jealousy? I hope not. Because I'm not jealous, right? Not in a possessive sense, I just find it rude that she flirt with him so blatantly when he's out with someone.

Grabbing my glass of water, I take a long thought-cleansing drink. "So, if it's not an ad you're selling, how are you going to help me find whatever it is you think I'm looking for?"

"I have my ways."

I lean in close and whisper, "I think they call them sources in your business."

"I have plenty of those too."

"Did these sources tell you I'm looking for something?"

"In a manner of speaking."

So speak, damn it. I'm getting the feeling he doesn't know shit, this is just a giant fishing expedition. One that's going to leave him with an empty hook, because I'm not taking his bait. Two can play beat around the bush. "And you speak so well."

He smiles, leaning back in his chair with a casual grace rarely seen in big men. "So tell me, Keely, what would you like me to help you find?"

A plate of sugary goodness fills the space between us, followed by two spoons. The scent alone is laden with a week's worth of calories.

It's not every day you can say you were saved by dessert. "I think I've figured out what you need to help me find."

His attempt to appear nonchalant is canceled out by the eager spark in his eyes. "Yes?"

I scrape my spoon through the caramel and ice cream covered pudding, then raise it to my lips. "My willpower." I slide the spoon inside my mouth.

His attention switches from my words to my actions, Adam's apple bobbing and a quick darting of his tongue across his lips.

The delicious feeling of achievement is even more satisfying than the sticky sweetness tantalizing my tastebuds. Damn, that was exhilarating. I've never played the seductress before, never thought I could pull it off, but after his reaction I might have to revisit the role. Without a doubt, it worked to my advantage in throwing him off his game.

Removing the spoon from my mouth is almost as much fun as putting it in. I make sure to slide it slowly between my lips and then lick them clean. "You're right, it's very good."

His jaw clenches as he swallows, lids sliding down in a slow blink. "What?"

"The pudding, it's wonderful. You'd better have some before I finish it all."

Haydn stabs his spoon in with a little more force than necessary. Shoving the contents into his mouth, he nods, careful to keep his eyes averted as he chews. "Yes, yes, it's great."

There's nothing like a little dessert to make all your problems go away.

Chapter 53

Sometimes I long for the simple days of phones without all the bells and whistles, but modern technology does have it's perks. Like the immediacy of knowing who's on the other end. Haven't had my coffee yet, and dealing with Var, his demands, and insecurities… that's a two pot situation, but what are ya gonna do, ignore a call from your boss? "What can I do for you, Var?"

"I heard that you had another date with Haydn Koehler."

Don't know why he needs me, he seems to have plenty of spies. "Yeah, he took me to dinner, before work last night."

"Did you learn anything?"

"He likes his steak medium well, takes sour cream with his baked potato, and loves bread pudding." Boy, does he love bread pudding, but I'll keep that to myself.

"Did he say anything that would point to why he is slandering me in his paper?"

Good grief, we're back to high school antics, proof that the female populace doesn't hold a monopoly on gossip and petty backbiting. "No, did you want me to come right out and ask?"

"Do not be foolish. He would know right away I sent you."

Like he doesn't already. Geez, get your giant head out of your ass. I'm glad we're chatting on the phone since my eye roll would make matters worse. Haydn's not a stupid man, but neither is Var. Until his vanity gets in the way.

"Then back off," I say. "Things like this take time. He's not going to confide in me right away, we barely know each other. I've got to build up some sort of trust."

"There are other ways of getting the information I desire."

"Such as?" I know what's coming, I've read too many books and seen to many movies not to know.

"You could search his office."

"When and how do you suggest I do this? I'm hardly qualified as a cat-burglar, I don't pick locks, or have the ability to hide from security cameras. There's no way Haydn is stupid enough to leave sensitive materials lying around for me to just stumble across. And before you can ask, I'm not a hacker. I know enough about computers to get by." Wow, can't believe I got all that out without one interruption.

"Then use what is at your disposal, the shadows."

Should have seen that coming. "You've witnessed what I've *mastered* in shadow craft, and it doesn't include using them to pick up items."

"Verein—"

The room darkens, shadows slither toward me as my anger reaches out to them. "For the last frickin' time, I'm not Einen. If you want Einen, go get him. I'm sure you know where he's at."

"I do not need Vereinen, I have you."

Go ahead, finish the sentence, ya frickin' asshat, 'to do my dirty work.' Taking a deep breath I push the shadows back into the corners and close the door on my anger. "Then you're going to have to be patient, I'm still learning."

"Speaking of, how is your training coming along?"

"You should probably ask Ric and Teiran. I'm not the best judge when it comes to that."

"Have you been practicing your Talents?"

He knows damn well I've been practicing. I wish he'd quit with the mundane small talk and get to the point. "Is there something important you need to ask me? If not, I'm kind of busy."

"When are you seeing him again?"

"If you mean Haydn, tonight."

"You are seeing an awful lot of Mr. Koehler."

"I thought that was my assignment."

"Your assignment is to find out what he is planning."

"Right now his plans include taking me to dinner and to a Health Care fundraiser." With everything Haydn's printed about his insurance coverage for Enchants, or lack of, that should get his goat.

"Do not forget who you work for, you are my Shadow, not his."

The line goes dead, just like my patience. Had I been smart, I would have sent him to voicemail and dealt with the fallout later. I didn't exactly help my situation with the heavy dose of sarcasm at the end, but he sure has his panties in a wad over Haydn taking me to dinner.

Is it possible Var is jealous of the time I'm spending with Haydn? Nah, it's not jealousy, not in the traditional sense. It's the idea of someone else playing with his toys. Var has the need to assert himself whenever and wherever he can. It's frickin' childish and annoying. I need a vacation from my new job.

I also need to get a dress for the big party. Who knew playing spy would mean I'd get to dress like a Bond girl? Dara is probably the better choice when it comes to picking out spy girl formal wear. Nyssa would have me in glitter and sequins and pretty much nothing else, not exactly weapons friendly.

Not that I think I'll need the shears, but it was decided—not by me, never by me—I have them with me at all times. 'What is the use of learning to use them if you do not have them with you?' Famous Teiran quote of the week, every week. Too bad he and the others can't get it through their heads that I don't want to use them. Not in the way they want me to, at least. I shiver, imagining shoving the sharp blades through flesh. All the blood. Using my Talents is messy enough, but I'm not the one with blood on my hands, not in the literal sense.

Chapter 54

I used to love the Mall, but I was a teen then, and they were shinny and new. Back then, there was nothing better than hanging out, gawking and gossiping, while sipping Orange Julius.

Shopping is only fun when you really want to be there and right now I don't. I'd much rather be in bed, hiding under the covers, dreaming of the gorgeous gown that's going to eat up a month's profits. Having to shell out that kind of money for one night hurts. It hurts like the tiny cuts leftover from over-zealous texturizing, compounded by spilled perm solution.

We'd already tried the secondhand stores, but alas that Mall walking, Orange Julius sipping girl is no more. I need something more suited to my age, not the flamboyant prom dresses I would have worn in a heartbeat. Of course, I wouldn't have made it to prom, The Sisters would have locked me in my room. And probably rightfully so. Damn, I am old. You'll probably catch me shouting 'damn kids, get off my lawn,' sooner than later.

"What about this one?" Nyssa holds out a lovely scrap of material with a V neckline cut to the bellybutton and slits to the hips on either side.

Dara shakes her head. "The slits are too high to conceal her weapon."

Funny how different our thought processes are, I was worried about it concealing my underwear. It goes back on the rack and I wander over to Rey, sliding hangers and mumbling, "No. No. No."

"Any luck?"

"No, I still like the silver lamé sheath."

"Yeah, I like the cut, but not the fabric." I'm kinda leaning toward Rey's picks, classy but sexy. We just need to find something that will meet Dara's weapon-worthy approval.

"But you've got to admit it looked amazing on you, and it had the appropriate slit for easy dagger access."

"It didn't hang right, I'd have people wondering about the bulge in my dress all night."

"A little higher and to the left and you'd really leave an impression."

"I don't need that kind of attention, I don't need any kind of attention. I want to kind of blend in with the background."

"With your date, that's never going to happen. It's damn near as bad as going out with Var Royd."

He's got me there. All of my recent 'dates' have drawn unwanted attention. Hel, even going anywhere with my partners gets every woman in a six mile radius hot, bothered, and ready to commit murder to be in my shoes. If they only knew, what I know.

"What about this one?" He holds what looks like a black Hefty bag with sleeves and I shake my head.

"Oh, hels no."

"It will look better on you than the hanger."

I give him 'the look' and he laughs.

"Come on, just try it. I promise it won't be as bad as you think." He places a hand at the small of my back and pushes me toward the dressing rooms.

And he's right, it's worse. Too bad my shopping buddies don't agree.

"Perfect," declares Dara, circling me like a hawk.

Nysa nods. "Not bad at all."

Rey gives me that 'I told you so' grin.

"You guys can't be serious? I look like I just walked off the set of Dynasty."

"A very popular and classy show," he says.

I glare at him. "Yeah, in the '80's." Turning to the mirror, I shake my head. "Look at these shoulder pads."

Rey stands behind me, his hands sliding from my massive shoulders to my waist. "They give the illusion of a tiny waist. And this"—he fluffs the excess material at my hips that tapers into a straight line falling to the floor—"completes the hourglass figure."

He's right, it gives me curves, but I still don't like it. The extra material hangs like curtains at my hips. Wait. Fussing with it, I've discovered something exciting about this dress. There are pockets hidden in those drapes. Shoving my hands inside, I grin. "This means I don't have to worry about an evening bag."

Dara kneels, pulling the right pocket inside out. "Or a place to hide your weapon. We will open this and re-stitch it, so you can simply reach inside."

"No embarrassing granny panty flashes, if you have to go for your blade." Should have known Nyssa's only worry would be me flashing my underwear. Not that I wear granny panties, but anything comfortable or practical fits her definition.

Rey fusses with my hair, mumbling about pearls, as I turn in front of the three-way mirror. I'm more concerned with the plunging back—if I had a tramp stamp it would be on full display. It also means I can't wear a traditional bra. Guess I'll either be letting what little I have hang free, or breaking out the petals. There is nothing like ripping something akin to a Band-Aid off delicate skin at the end of the night.

Beauty is pain, pain is beauty.

Chapter 55

After encountering the illusions placed on Einen's home, I've got an inkling that Vana is on to me. There's no use going back, she'll only up her security. I have to believe Einen and his shadow minions are still trapped in the house, but otherwise unharmed. What I need to focus on is the key. With Haydn helping me out—still not sure what's in it for him, I may be dumb, but I'm not stupid—I have a fraction of extra time to spend finding it. Time I'll explain away as doing paperwork for the salon, if questioned by my overseers.

Teiran seems to think I should spend every second of every day either working out or practicing my Talents. Ric is a little more lenient, allowing me some free time to *rejuvenate*. Who the hel has time to rejuvenate? I'm lucky if I can sneak in a couple of hours of sleep, nothing rejuvenating about that, it just keeps me from collapsing.

A quick internet search shows me a multitude of ways to create a magical key. Every one of them relies on a vessel of some sort. The best vessel I can think of is her necklace, Brísingamen. Getting that away from her is a challenge I'm not cut out for since I don't have the skills of the Trickster. And why would she use it as her vessel when it's a source of her power? Surely the key's something else.

Maybe I need to confide in Haydn. His connections could get me information beyond my reach. And he seems to know I'm looking for something other than the obvious. Problem number one with that plan is giving him inside info on Var, which leads to problem number two, Var finding out and he will find out. There's no way Haydn's ego, combined with this vendetta against Var, will stop him from telling the world I told him.

Not a chance I'd ask Mort for help. Not only has he misrepresented himself, but he upped the chances of ratting me out to gain status in the Ahnenerbe Society. Plus, since Teiran and Ric know about him, they've probably added him to the watch list. Which makes me wonder if Var knows. Nah, if he did, he would have berated me for not telling him myself.

Even if I was tempted to make a deal with Stasia, she'd laugh in my face. Vana's already offered her the golden goose for nothing more than a cut of the profit. Why else would the two of them be working together? Makes me wonder how Teiran will take the news of the woman who had her claws on his best friend and the goddess he adores working together. Can I use this to my advantage?

I want to keep Nyssa and Rey out of it, and Dara… Dara would flip sides and guard the key to keep me from releasing Einen.

I am so out of options.

Rolling away from the computer, I get up and flop on the bed. If I were Vana, where would I hide the key? I keep coming back to that damn chunk of amber cradled in her cleavage. That's not the right answer, I know it's not. It's too freakin' easy. She had to have used something I'd never expect.

Maybe that's why she was chatting up Stasia at the coffee shop, to pass it to her. Nah, that would give someone else control, and I can't see Vana ever relinquishing control over anything, except maybe to her brother, but that's more of an indulgence than a total handover. She's still top dog, no matter how much he'd like to think otherwise.

If I could get inside her house… Yeah, that's brilliant, put yourself in her court. Like she'd keep it there anyway, knowing it was the first place I'd look.

Wish I could figure out what those blobs were, that Shadow Copy showed me. There's something about them that does and doesn't make sense. They have to be the key to finding *the* key. I'm thinking they had to be living beings and not shadow creatures. There were four of them. One was almost certainly Vana, the others could have been anyone. Var? Even if it was, he's the last person who would tell me anything, except to rub it in my face. If two of the usual suspects were the Wonder Twins, that would leave… Ric and Teiran. I guess it makes sense they would have their bodyguards along for the lockup. It also means I continue to live in the House of Screwed. There's no way in hel, those two will tell me what I need to know.

All of this brings me back to my informant, SC. Maybe chancing another trip isn't a bad idea after all. I need to look past the glamours and illusions and get inside the house. I may not find the answers I need, but I'll find something. At this point anything would be considered a win. Why am I wasting time thinking instead of doing?

Closing my eyes, I start with deep calming breaths, focusing on Einen's house. The entranceway to be exact, bypassing the outdoors and going right inside is the goal. I've done it before, why not try again? With one small caveat, this time I don't want to end up in Einen's bedroom. Not that her spells would let me, but if I did succeed, both of us trapped would kinda defeat the purpose.

I'm not sure if it's my location choice or if Vana's upped her game, but I feel like I'm crawling through thick, sticky goop. His house is there, I can see it, but it keeps moving just out of reach. The feeling of dread amplifies. My head begins to pound. Vision blurs. Limbs weigh a ton. But I'm getting closer, and the house is within reach. The door is under my fingertips. I grasp the knob. One last push, that's all I need. Stumbling forward, I fall into blackness.

Chapter 56

Ow, ow, ow, my frickin' head hurts, along with the rest of my body. Either I can't open my eyes or wherever I am is completely dark. Not a spark of light anywhere. Can't-see-your-hand-in-front-of-your-face dark. Did I make it into Einen's house? Rolling onto my hands and knees, I slowly crawl across stone, maybe marble. Yep, feels like the floor of his foyer.

Can Vana conjure absolute darkness? If not, I know who can. "Teiran."

A squeak of pain slips out as the tips of my fingers connect with something solid. I flex then wiggle them, they hurt, but aren't broken. Happy, happy. Joy, joy. Carefully, I reconnect my hand with the floor, sliding it toward the obstacle, then up and over the smooth finish. Stairs, I found the stairs. Not that I'm going up, but it gives me a little perspective of where I am in the room. Turning, I sit with my back against them, staring out into the nothingness. What I wouldn't give for a flashlight, or Dara's lighter. I don't even know if either would work in this kind of magic, but I'd sure give them a try.

"Well this was a giant fuckin' waste of time." Without any light, there are no shadows. No shadows, no questions. No questions, no answers. "Damn it."

Wonder if this how she's keeping Einen in his room, it would explain why the shadows were roaming the house. It's what I would do if I were in her shoes, keep him from using them. I'm starting to think it wasn't just Einen's Talents that drove him batshit, it was everything working against him. From Var's ego to Vana's fear he'd been working with Hel, it's no secret there's a special kind of animosity between them. The heady power that comes with commanding shadow and death was just the beginning. I'm surprised I'm still sane. Although, I'm questioning it right now, considering I'm sitting here and not on my way back to my body.

Cold fingers dance along my spine. Can I get home? I'm not sure if my being here has something to do with the shadows or is a completely different Talent.

"Now that you've got yourself totally freaked out, what're you gonna do about it?"

If it weren't so damn dark, it would be peaceful. The quiet, the solitude, it's kinda nice. A nice place to visit, wouldn't wanna live there, kind of nice. The darkness seems to strip away all your senses. It makes you feel small, insignificant, and alone.

Trapped in your own head. Yeah, being stuck here for long periods of time would drive anyone insane. Like The Between.

I'd been there once. Once is enough, I never want to experience it again. The Between is the place between worlds or realms, whatever you want to call them. As the name suggests it's everything and nothing, life and death, reality and fantasy, that empty yet full place between it all. From all accounts, most don't return and those who do are never the same. I have a feeling it's a lot like what Alice encountered when she fell down the rabbit hole.

I'm a between, a thing between light and dark. Maybe that's why I was able to leave with my mind intact. It changed me, but for better or worse? Hel tossed me into The Between, when I was trying to escape from The Collector. It was there I committed murder. By using my Talent to call upon the dead, I'd opened door to revenge, and his victims took him.

Better, because it forced me to stay alive. Worse, because I took justice into my own hands. And even worse yet, it felt good.

Dark places bring dark thoughts. Those dark thoughts ignite something tucked deep inside. Something I've tried to keep locked away, because once it's out, I don't know what it will do. What *I* will do, because that something is essentially me.

Everyone has a dark side, mine just happens to be cloaked in shadow and death. And it feels good.

It feels so good, the tightness and itch of my skin is a minor annoyance. I reach out into the darkness, grabbing it with metaphysical hands and pull it to me. Into me, absorbing it until the blackness of my surroundings begin to change. Sweat courses down my face, stinging my eyes. It coats my skin, aggravating the itch. As the color changes, from pure black to gradual variations of off-black, my body begins to shake. When it reaches a dim grey, the pain in every muscle, every joint weighs me down. My head is on the verge of exploding and tears mingle with sweat.

My subconscious reminds me that if I overextend myself, I may not make it home. But it's warnings fall on deaf ears.

I want this. I need this.

Want what? Need what?

I'll know it when I see it.

I can't pull any more darkness into me. Maintaining the grey begins to take its toll, sucking away what little strength I have left.

There in the distance, a form, a figure. It reaches out to me. Pictures, visions, and memories are pushed into my head. Not a one makes sense, my concentration is focused on holding back the dark. That hold becoming more and more unstable. The figure blurs, begins to fade, along with my strength. My head spins and my stomach empties. Blackness returns.

Chapter 57

Light, as dim as it is, blinds me. Shooting, sharp pain rips through my eyes and into my brain. It takes a moment or two to realize the pounding isn't just in my head, but on my door. Slowly, with much whining, I manage to sit up. Looking around through squinted eyes, I shake my head and immediately regret it. I'm one lucky little schattenkind. Soupy blackness one minute, my spare bedroom the next. No questioning, no bitching.

"Come on in," I shout, hoping to silence the knocking.

"Can't, it's locked," Rey answers.

That's right, I'd locked it so I could do whatever the hel I just did in private. "Be right there."

Sliding from the bed, I stand still, or as still as one can when the room is spinning. A headache, the flu, exhaustion? I'll use whatever excuse I can, don't want anyone knowing what happened. Dizziness somewhat under control, I tap the power button on the computer monitor. No use taking chances.

The hall is easily navigated, using the walls as

support. The living room is a little more difficult, with too many things threatening to trip me up, including a cat. Cramped fingers fiddle with the deadbolt and it takes both hands to get it turned. Thank the gods, I didn't set the chain. I'm not sure I could get it out of the slot. The doorknob—I'll leave that to Rey.

"Come on in." The door swings open as I shuffle my way to the couch.

"What took you so long? Why'd you lock the door?"

I hold up a hand after lowering myself gingerly into the cushions. "One question at a time, please. And could you use your inside voice?"

He takes a seat on the edge of the coffee table. "What's going on? Are you okay?" Leaning toward me, he reaches out and presses a hand to my forehead. "You're warm. Are you sick?"

"Everybody's warm, it's August in Iowa." I push his hand away. "It's just a headache."

"Well you better get over it, girl. You've got a party to get ready for."

Shit, I'd forgotten the damn Health Care thingamabob. "How about my dress? Is it ready?"

"Yeah, Dara got it all stitched up nice and neat. No one will know you're packing' unless you play show and tell. She also adjusted one of her thigh holsters for you."

"You make it sound like I'm going to a shootout

at the O.K. Corral instead of a fundraiser for health care."

"One never can tell with you along for the ride, pardner. Now giddy up and let's get your hair done."

"Think I'll take something for this headache first."

"Knowing you, it's probably caffeine withdrawal. Might want to grab a gallon to wash 'em down with."

I nod, and regret it straightaway. "Can't hurt." At least not like my body and head do. So not looking forward to having Rey yank on my hair. Maybe I can talk him into something simple without thousands of stabbing bobby pins.

"Meet you downstairs." He exits stage left, leaving me to stumble my way to the kitchen.

"Wow, I've got to get my shit together or tonight will be even more *fun* than expected." I'll look like a comedy act, stumbling on heels, tripping on the hem of my dress… you name it, it's bound to happen. Hel, I might even throw up in the punchbowl. Do they have punchbowls at fancy things like this? Doesn't matter. All that matters is the six-pack of Dr. Pepper in the fridge and a prescription dose of ibuprofen. And a shower.

I'd rather sit and reflect on what happened in Einen's house, but it's going to have to wait until I get home. My fear is that it will fade before I get the chance to review and digest. If I could only decipher what Shadow Copy—the form had to be him—was trying to show me. The thought of trying to break it all down makes my head and shoulders throb. So I stop thinking and position myself under the water, letting it beat away the pain.

Four little pills, half a can of soda, and a deep tissue massage by water works wonders. Life feels doable again as I hurry down to get my hair done. The salon isn't open yet, so we have it all to ourselves. I'm feeling a little guilty leaving Dara and Rey to fend for themselves tonight, especially with the added load of my clients who didn't want to reschedule. I count my blessings— understanding clients and good friends. It helped that I'm going to a charity event. Nobody wants to appear uncharitable.

I slide into Rey's chair and he eyes my bathrobe. "Want a cape on?"

"Nah, you're not cutting anything."

He runs his fingers through my hair. "Thanks for not washing it, makes it easier."

"Duh."

"Oh, that's right, you do hair too." He grins at me in the mirror. "What are we doing?"

"Something simple, to go with the dress. Nothing piled on top of my head, don't think I could take the weight or pins stabbing me right now."

"Okay, how about if you Godiva it for me, so it's past your butt? We'll do a long side braid over your shoulder, weave in some strands of ribbon and maybe some beads? Simple, elegant and totally shocking when they get an eyeful of that plunging back."

"No beads, no ribbon, just the braid."

His lower lip protrudes. "You're no fun."

"And Nys wears pouty mouth better. I want to stay as simple and off the radar as possible."

"Then I guess you won't be down with the temporary tattoo I found for your back."

"Umm, no tramp stamps."

"Fine, old school elegance it is."

The disappointment is an act, old Hollywood glam is Rey's forte and nobody does it better. Hence his clientele of ladies of a certain age. I'd bet money that he's planning on reinventing the look once that generation fades. I've seen some of the creations he's done on the younger set and the popularity is gaining. It doesn't hurt that Rey is a fox. And I don't mean just his therian heritage of being able to shift into one. Waist length auburn hair, forest colored eyes, and cheekbones to die for make him easy on the eyes. That slight Cajun drawl that shows up when he's flirting or angry just adds to the mystic. He's quite the specimen. Just not my type of specimen, but it doesn't mean I can't appreciate his beauty.

Or his work. Damn, my hair looks fantastic, even

if I did have to expend a little energy to get the length he needed. I even like the little jeweled band he used to secure the ends, it will sparkle nicely against the black of my dress.

"A touch of lipstick and some mascara, and they won't be able to keep their eyes off you."

Not exactly what I was going for, but I think my days of flying under the radar are over.

Chapter 58

It may not be the luxury of a limo, but Haydn's car isn't a clunker either. As a mater of fact, I prefer it to the limo, but I'm always going to pick a muscle car over anything else on the road. With the exception of the Camaro. No, just no.

"Maybe I should have driven the SUV."

"Hel, no," I say, gathering my dress around me as I climb into his Challenger. "I mean, this is fine."

His laughter draws all eyes toward us as he close my door and walks around to his side. "That hel, no, tells me it's more than fine."

I shrug. "What can I say? I appreciate a car that rumbles and can smoke the tires."

"A muscle car girl, huh?"

"Yep, remind me to show you mine sometime."

He looks a little surprised. "You have a muscle car?"

"Yeah, something wrong with that?"

"You never cease to surprise me. What do you have?"

"A '69 Mustang convertible."

A low appreciative whistle fills the car. "Nice. Speaking of, you look exceptionally nice."

I shoot him a smile. "You clean up pretty well, yourself."

He does look impressive. And that tux has to be custom made. There's no way it came off the rack, not with the way it fits.

"I forgot to ask, where is this shindig?"

"Downtown, at the Convention Center."

"They must be expecting a big crowd."

"Everybody who's anybody will be there."

Between his words and the car's acceleration as he guns it onto 141, my stomach gets left in The Meadows. Everybody who's anybody. That everybody is sure to include my boss.

"Great, sounds like my kind of party."

He sighs and I wish I would have dialed back the scorn.

"I didn't mean it to come out like—

"Don't worry about it, I should have told you sooner. To be honest, I was afraid you'd turn me down."

As much as I'd like to agree with him, I know I would have forced myself to say yes. It would have raised too many red flags in my story if he showed up without me. "No, I still would have said yes."

"Because you wanted to go, or because Var Royd will be there."

"Honestly, a little of both. I like spending time with you and not going would have tipped him off that my reports are a sham."

"If you don't mind me asking, what have you been telling him?"

I do mind, but not because I think he's pumping me for info on Var. I know he's doing that, he always tries to get a tidbit or two. I mind because I don't want him to laugh at me, or get ideas about us. "I kinda implied that we are... dating."

Yep, laughter. "And he fell for it?"

"Seems too, but I'm going to have to come up with something on you to appease him soon. He's getting itchy."

"I think we can come up with a tantalizing bit of intel that won't cause too much trouble. Man, I love messing with him. It's almost more satisfying than the thought of ruining him financially."

Is that what he's up to? Trying to ruin Var financially? I'd like to believe I just caught a bit of info that wasn't supposed to be said, but Haydn's tricky. He could have tossed that out there just to see if I would bite.

"As long as we're all having fun."

He glances over at me and winks. "Well, I don't know about you, but I've been having the time of my life."

I hope my smile doesn't look forced, but now he's got me worried. Please don't step into relationship land, I don't want to go anywhere near the border. "So, are you at this party as the crème de la crème or in a journalistic capacity?"

"Little of both. How about you? Are you there as a spy or just my date?"

"Oh, a little of both."

Thankfully, he laughs. "Should be a good time on all levels."

That all depends on your definition of a good time. I just want this night to be over, without any complications. But with my luck, you can count on there being complications.

When he pulls into a line of cars in front of the Convention Center, I'm relieved. I'd been dreading hiking to our destination in heels. Valet parking. Ahh, life is good when you hang with the crème de la crème.

A smiling young man in a red vest opens my door, holding out a hand. Placing mine in his, I gather my dress with the other, swing my legs out, and he pulls me to my feet. Woohoo, I didn't fall flat on my face, or catch my heel in the hem of my dress. So far, so good, but I still have steps to tackle. Haydn tosses the keys to the boy, grabs my hand, and wraps it around his arm. Luckily, I have a strong arm to lean on.

Slipping his invitation from his jacket, Haydn hands it to a man who scans it and waves us through. I'm not sure what I expected, but this looks like any other banquet I've attended, except people are dressed fancier. It's like a mash-up of red carpet dreams and a salon awards ceremony.

We just dress a little wilder, or more casually, take your pick. Pretty much anything goes.

"There are a lot of people here," I whisper, tightening my grip on his arm.

He pats my hand. "Everyone cares about health care. Don't worry, they won't bite, but be careful. Some of these *ladies* have claws. Like the blonde across the room."

My eyes follow his nod. Damn it, I could have gone all night without seeing Vana Royd. To be fair, Haydn warned me Var would be here, and where Var goes, Vana follows. She gives me a smirk and half wave. I'm in polite company so I do the polite thing and nod, when what I want to do is flip her the bird.

"Don't let her get to you." The warmth of his hand settles on small of my back—bare back—directing me into the crowd.

He's right, but it's too late, she got to me a long time ago.

"I'm going to get us something to drink. Any special requests?"

"I wouldn't mind something bubbly."

"Bubbly it is. Back in a minute."

The warmth is gone from my back, leaving me feeling suddenly vulnerable. I didn't realize how much having him at my side helped in dealing with this crowd.

People ebb and flow around me, until a

familiar face passes by. "Karen? Karen Engle?" I say, catching her gaze.

"Keely." She stops, her expression fluctuating from happy-to-see-you to I'd-rather-be-anywhere-else.

"H—how are you?" What the hel do you say to someone who's career had been destroyed? Who's life had been destroyed? Who's Talent's had been taken? Not how are you, that's for sure. Karen had been my client, but that had ended when The Collector had taken her hands and with them, her Talent to heal.

"Fine, and you?"

"The same."

"Look, Keely, I don't blame you, I just can't..."

"I understand." I move to place my hand over what should have been her hand. Hel's Realm, I'm stepping in everything tonight. "I—gods, Karen, I'm sorry."

"Don't worry about it, it takes some getting used to."

"Is there anything they can do for you?"

"They're working on some special prosthetics for me. Of course they can't give me back my..."

"What about your job?"

"I was lucky there, they always need more pencil pushers. Of course I have someone else to push it while I dictate."

"I wish—"

"It was good seeing you, Keely." She smiles, an empty, sad smile and walks away.

Chapter 59

A glass of sparkling bubbles dangles from large fingers and I grab it, nearly knocking back the contents in one swig.

"That was Karen Engle, wasn't it?"

I nod.

"She was one of your clients, right?"

"Yep, you know the story. The Collector took her hands. Your reporters covered it. Covered my shop too."

"We were just doing our job."

"Making my life a living hel by surrounding my building and not giving me a moment's peace? That was your job?"

"Hey, hey, I didn't mean to dredge up bad memories. And I certainly didn't mean to make your life a living hel. The only excuse I have is the one you've already heard."

I set the empty champagne flute on a passing tray. I'm doing my best to rein in my anger before something very unfortunate happens. The last thing I need right now is to add to the mystique of the infamous Schattenkind by letting loose in a room full of money and influence.

"Reporters are assholes, you're hearing it from a credible source."

I glance up at him.

"Come on, not even a glimmer of a smile?"

"Not really in a smiling mood."

"You might want to rethink that. Your boss is watching." He tips his head to the right.

Great. Var raises his glass toward me, a big ol' shit-eating grin on his face. What the hel has he got to smile about? Oh, that's right, I'm doing his dirty work. Again my middle finger itches, but Haydn's hand encompasses it and the rest of my fingers.

"Careful now, we don't want to give him a reason to come over here."

"True."

"How about we discuss what I can do to make the past up to you?"

The warmth returns to the small of my back as he turns me toward the dance floor. With my hand still in his, he pulls me close, and beings swaying to the music. My only choice is to follow along if I don't want to draw any more attention.

"What do you have in mind?" It can't be any worse than Var's sorry, not sorry, flowers.

"Oh, I think I hold the key to all your problems."

Key? Son of a—how does he know about the key? Or is it just a turn of phrase? Am I over thinking this? Then again, did I actually expect him not to snoop on me?

"I know what you've been searching for."

"I don't know what you mean. I'm not searching for anything, except dirt on you."

His laughter draws smiles and stares from every direction. Trying to maintain a friendly distance within whisper range is more difficult than it looks. Especially, when I see how my boss staring. Even if Haydn doesn't get the wrong idea about us, Var will jump to conclusions.

"Silly girl, tricks are for Tricksters."

"Are you claiming the title?"

"No, but a little may have rubbed off over the years."

"What are you getting at?"

He spins me so I'm facing away from him. Locking me in his arms he leans down, his breath warm against my ear. "Hopefully, you."

I mange to slip from his grasp and turn to face him. "You've got an answer for everything, don't you?"

"I try, now back to the subject at hand." His playful smile and attitude slips away. "I know what you're looking for and I want to help."

With the grace and fitness of a much smaller man, he spins me out and back, leaving me off kilter and a little breathless.

"How do you know?"

"I'm a journalist, remember?"

"So you've been snooping on me."

"Oh, fire and brimstone, woman, I'm trying to help you."

"Fine, if you truly know, then you also know this isn't the place to discuss it."

"Not for deep discussion of the subject, too many people get antsy when they hear that name."

"But not you."

Cradling me in his arm, he lowers me until my braid is pooled on the floor, his face hovering just above mine. He simply smiles in response, then lifts me, holding tight until I regain my balance.

"Should we leave and discuss this over a cup of coffee?"

"Leaving when we just arrived? That would raise too many brows. No, we have to stay a little longer."

"You're playing me."

"No, no I'm not, but they are." Haydn nods in the direction of Var and his entourage.

I can't tell if Var's pleased, displeased, or indifferent to the show Haydn's giving him. The set of his jaw and clenched hands, tells me Ric's not pleased and I feel a butterfly or two of exhilaration. Teiran, on the other hand, stares at me with a burning intensity that hits me like a gut punch. Vana, well, she's Vana, flirting with anything on two legs. She doesn't even look in my direction.

"Tell me something I don't know."

"Two of them are what you're looking for, I'll let you guess which two."

The floor drops and I'm thankful for Haydn's arms around me as the visions SC pressed into my mind come tumbling back. Four blobby shapes outside Einen's room. One stands in the distance. Two press their hands against the door, while the third holds their other hands. Dark and light swirl and entwine, covering the door. The two fall to their knees, dangling from the other's grasp. Light, brilliant and bright twirls about the trio, in a mingling of every color of the imagination. Their auras, power, whatever, come together in a blinding flash.

And so do all the pieces. The key isn't a something, it's a someone, or in this case two someones. Vana has turned the Sword and Shield into the Key.

Acknowledgments

There is no one I'd like to thank more than my fans. You have stuck with me through thick and thin.

Next up I have to thank my amazing editor, Tamara Jones, she showed me the way and held my hand through it all. My beta-readers, the Saturday Writers, and the amazing writers I call friends, you guys and gals are awesome. A special thank you to Dennis Green for standing in my corner and cheering me on.

Last, but not least, my family and friends.

About the Author

A.R. Miller writes urban fantasy for grown-ass women (and men) who are still too young to care.

She lives in Iowa with an accommodating husband and their four-footed companions. When not testing the patience of readers with cliffhanger endings, you might find her wielding a makeup brush or curling iron as a freelance stylist.

To find out more about A.R. or the Fey Creations series, visit www.feycreations.com.